BAD GIRL DILEMMA

LESSONS IN DOMINANCE

ZARA COX

Copyright © 2025 by Zara Cox

All rights reserved.

No part of this book may be reproduced in any form or by any electronic or mechanical means, including information storage and retrieval systems, without written permission from the author, except for the use of brief quotations in a book review.

CHAPTER 1

Dahlia

Not gonna lie, this is my favorite part.

Okay, maybe not my *absolute* favorite.

But watching pollsters on my heavily encrypted social media app lose their minds always gives me a buzz.

I watch two contenders battle it out until it hits the 85% mark, then the fickle public, as they always do, rallies behind one.

Tonight's clear winner hits 92%, and I grin.

Obsidian Corp it is.

I don't use the actual entity names beforehand, of course, because that would be stupid.

Obsidian is only known as 'Triple D' to my pollsters.

Lying on my stomach in bed, legs tangled in my sheets, chin propped on one hand, I wait for the stragglers to get on board. I like to get as close to 100% as I can.

There's a delayed gratification to that—a sizzling in my

veins that comes with righteous sinning. That's a high I like to skate as long as possible. Forget drugs, it comes as close to sex as I can get.

So while the disgruntled few whose initial picks didn't make the cut make up their minds, I swipe lazily across the screen.

The poll numbers spike in real time. Thousands of anonymous voices weighing in on who deserves a taste of my justice.

My fingers hover over the voting breakdown.

Each name on the list makes my blood boil.

✦ A billionaire hedge fund vampire who crashed a housing market for sport.

✦ A pharmaceutical exec who jacked insulin prices mid-pandemic and is still at it.

✦ A prince with offshore accounts full of human trafficking money.

✦ Triple D, founder of "O" Corp, crypto king, rumored sadist, silent investor in all the above.

The comments under his name are extra spicy.

"That Triple D guy gives me the creeps."

"Didn't his bio say he blackmailed a journalist into disappearing?"

"Such a shame he's fuck-hot. Or is it??!"

"Do him and I'll tattoo your name on my ass."

I chuckle. My followers are feral, and I love them for it.

I'm no saint. I've never claimed to be. But there's something delicious about righteous vengeance dressed in latex and filtered through a voice modulator. I steal. I expose. I redistribute. I livestream it all. And if I get a little thrill watching corrupt assholes rage and lose their minds as they promise to hunt me down and "insert extremely unimaginative punishment of choice here"—also, dream on, fuckers? *Bonus.*

When I hit 96%, I flip onto my back, flick out of the poll and swipe to another app. Just to... peek. I may be putting the proverbial cart before the horse, but I'm already dreaming up ways to reward myself once I'm done notching another win under my belt.

The Club app opens in full dark mode, purring like a secret lover.

It was a joke at first—signing up. A little curiosity, a little mischief. I never expected to keep it. But somehow, logging on after a job has become a ritual, although tonight I'm doing it before, not after. Which, if I believed in superstition, I would be fucked. But I don't, so...

I don't talk much on the app. Just... watch. Explore. I've interacted a couple of times, but mostly I've created dirty little fantasies in my head I secretly hope will come true.

Dominants, subs, contracts, scenes.

Intimacy without strings.

Pain twisted into pleasure.

There's something almost reverent about it. Like control isn't something you seize—but something you surrender.

Maybe after this job, I'll finally do what I've been too chicken to do so far and... indulge. Dip my toe in the water, so to speak. I don't know how far I'll get because all that surrendering sounds copasetic in theory, but yeah... I'm not the surrendering type.

Maybe a clean, anonymous hookup. No feelings. Just breathless, beautiful pain. A reward for a job well done. I scan a few profiles, half-distracted. A masked man with a wicked mouth.

That Dom with blood-red leather gloves. The one I keep returning to over and over.

My pulse flutters. I take note of his name.

SinMadeFlesh. Meh, not exactly original, but whatever.

Maybe I'll message him. Later.

I shut down the app and return to the poll.

98%. That's as good as I'm going to get.

I roll off the bed, energy spiking at the prospect of vengeance.

Showtime.

* * *

My gear is already laid out: matte black cargo pants, tight turtleneck, harness strapped with micro-tools, soundless boots. My gloves are fingerprint-resistant, and my mask—sleek and mirrored—covers half my face, voice modulator built into the jawline.

I secure my ponytail, zip everything up, and look at myself in the mirror.

No one would guess I'm twenty-two. That I'm very partial to cereal for dinner, and cry during Pixar shorts. That I once built a server farm in my mom's garage to DDOS a revenge-porn site.

All they see is Specter—digital thief, vigilante brat, chaos in motion.

Not Dahlia Wynn, cybersecurity expert and programmer.

I tap the go-live button. "Specter, online."

My voice comes out distorted, laced with static and steel. The screen flashes green. My viewers spike fast.

"Yessss she's back."

"This one's gonna be juicy, I can feel it."

"Who's tonight's victim, Specter?"

"You voted. I listened. It's Triple D," I purr. "Let's rob the devil."

* * *

BAD GIRL DILEMMA

The building looms like a monolith, all Obsidian glass and silent menace as if its owner were reflecting the city, daring it to come closer.

I slip inside like smoke—through a service entrance, past sleeping cameras, under the pulse of motion sensors I've already looped. My custom drone buzzes softly at my side, flashing green when the path is clear.

Heart rate steady. Breathing controlled. No fear. I'm in the zone.

Until the actual heist, all I'll be charged with on the *extreme off chance* I'm caught is corporate trespassing: a slap on the wrist, a fine, or some community service. Totally worth it.

But I don't plan on getting caught.

Obsidian has the honor of being my introduction into double-digit heisting, and I've been doing this for two years.

Up ten floors. Through the server vault. Past biometric locks. My custom key slips into the panel, and I wait for the soft chime of access granted.

Ding.

I grin under the mask. Too fucking easy.

I plug in, fingers flying, siphoning encrypted data through my proxy chains, dumping it into blockchain wallets faster than a heartbeat.

The stream's eating it up. Comments fly.

"Holy shit, she's in."

"That's Triple D's master key, isn't it??"

"Fuck, five mil. Six! Gah, seven and a half!"

"You're on fire, Spec! Get it, girl!"

"GET OUT GET OUT—"

Wait. Something's wrong.

The files… they're looping. Duplicating. I blink.

INTRUSION DETECTED. TRACE IN PROGRESS.

Reverse beacon triggered.

User: SPECTER
Location: LOGGED
Protocol: Velvet Vice Fingerprint Activated.
Cold drips into my veins. My drone flashes red.
What. The. Fuck.
No.
My breath strangles in my throat. I yank the drive, slam my laptop closed, kill the stream.

How did he—?

I've barely been here five minutes. To react this fast, he'd have to have known, have to have been lying in wait.

How the *fuck* did he know? Every piece of equipment I use is encrypted. Designed by me because I trust no one else in this world. Life lessons learned the hard way.

A voice slides through the earpiece. Not mine. Not filtered. Smooth. Male. Lethal.

"You shouldn't have been so sloppy, little thief."

I freeze.

There's no fucking way. I wasn't sloppy. I fucking wasn't.

The voice continues, low and wicked, right in my skull. "But I'm glad you were. I've been waiting for you."

CHAPTER 2

Dahlia

The smell hits me first.

Leather. Oil. The faintest trace of something metallic—blood? No. Don't go there.

I come to in darkness. Cramped, my arms twisted painfully behind my back, wrists bound tight with some kind of zip cord. There's a gag in my mouth—thick, padded, invasive. My jaw aches.

I try to scream, but it's strangled. Pathetic.

My face presses into something plush and cold. The thrum of a car engine vibrates under my cheek, and the realization slams into me like a bullet train. The shadow looming toward me, the leather-clad hand holding the dark cloth.

I'm in the trunk of a car.

I've been kidnapped.

A garbled sound pushes against the gag. Had it escaped, I'm sure it would sound a cross between laughter and shocked tears. *Hystericry*.

In a way I'm glad I don't get to hear it because…

No. No, no. *No.*

This isn't how it's supposed to go.

I've always been careful. Always five steps ahead. No paper trail. No biometric residue. Every signal bounced through so many proxies it would take a government weeks to catch up. And yet—here I am.

Tied up. Silenced. On my way to what… being disappeared?

Who the fuck did this? Who has the tech—no, the *nerve*—to turn my own heist on me?

My mind flashes through possibilities like a Rolodex on fire. The Vesper Syndicate? That slimeball senator I bankrupted last month? Maybe it's—

Like acid rain, everything I've learned of the owner of Obsidian both on and off the Dark Web drizzles through my mind.

And with each recollection, panic claws at my throat, but I force it down.

Think, Dahlia. *Think.*

But the name my mind keeps circling back to pulses through me like a detonation.

Dante 'Devil' O'Driscoll. Triple D.

I hacked him. Livestreamed it. Laughed. I didn't use his name, but somehow the bastard knew. He was waiting. Here in New York instead of on the other side of the country, and apparently not where my superior surveillance said he should be. Dammit.

God, what will he do to me? Interrogation? Torture? Worse?

A wave of nausea rolls through me, fast and violent. I squeeze my eyes shut.

Don't cry. Don't shake. Don't give them that.

I think of my mother—just for a second. The way her fingers used to dance over her laptop keyboard, fierce and bright and fearless. She was a truth-seeker. Until they silenced her.

The memory slices too close to bone. I shove it away.

What would Dad think if he knew where I was? That his daughter, his little digital prodigy, was bound and gagged in the back of some psycho's trunk? Will they tell him what happened to me? Do I want them to?

Or would it be better if I simply disappeared off the face of the earth? Because one death is bad enough. Two deaths of the people he loves in one lifetime…

God. Breathe.

I inhale through my nose, slow and steady, counting heartbeats like code lines.

And then—

The car slows.

Stops.

A door slams. Then another. Muffled voices. Footsteps.

A click. The sound of the trunk latch popping. Light spills in, blinding and surgical.

I blink, squinting through the gag, and then—

Him.

The man himself. Dante O'Driscoll. In the flesh.

Towering. Black suit. Blacker eyes. Shadow-cut jaw and cheekbones carved by God on a hate bender. There's a rawness to him that feels barely leashed—like he could destroy something with a flick of his wrist and wouldn't even flinch.

Even though I'd suspected, a part of me had hoped it wasn't him. That he would be someone less… formidable. Less potent. Less… just *less*.

That the single image I'd found on him online would be severely photoshopped, the kind that turned troll into hunk. Sadly, he's Online Hunk turned Hotter Hunk IRL.

His expression is unreadable. No smile. No mockery. Just

controlled fury, burning behind cold black eyes. For an abstract, entirely inappropriate moment I wonder if he named his company after the color of his eyes.

He looks down at me like I'm a piece of art he doesn't know whether to sell or smash.

And then, he speaks—his voice smooth, low, lethal.

"You really should've deleted that app, little thief."

The app...the app...The Club app?

Oh shit...

Oh fucking fuckity fuck!

* * *

Dante

SHE'S SMALLER than I expected.

Curled up like a snapped violin string, trying so hard not to tremble. I see it anyway. The twitch of her thigh. The flex of her bound wrists. The jagged inhale through her nose, because her mouth's stuffed full of premium-grade silicone that muffles all her screams.

She's scared.

Good.

She fucking should be.

I watch her carefully, silently, as she blinks against the light, trying to square the woman she stole from with the one standing in front of her.

What was she expecting? Some crusty billionaire with a temper, bald combover and a security detail?

Not me.

Not the man who knew exactly what kind of deviant little secret she was hiding behind that screen. Not the one who reverse-engineered her location using the very app she used to get off anonymously. Not the man who studied her browsing habits on The Club app and read her filthy, aching little wish list like it was a love letter to her own undoing.

She has no idea who she's dealing with. How long I've been waiting.

For today.

For her.

CHAPTER 3

Dahlia

His goons drag me into some kind of private elevator—luxury, glass, too clean for blood but not for power. My wrists are still bound. The gag's gone, but my mouth is dry. I haven't said a word.

I won't give him the satisfaction of my voice or my begging.

Dante O'Driscoll stands inches from me, tall and silent in his black-on-black suit, watching me the way a wolf might watch a dying deer: amused, lazily stretching out the time before delivering the death blow.

His presence is… overwhelming.

It's not just that he's gorgeous—though he is. More beautiful than any man should be, all sharp cheekbones and dark stubble and sinful lips that probably only curl when he's breaking something. Or someone.

It's the *stillness* that makes my pulse skitter. The contained threat.

BAD GIRL DILEMMA

Like he's constantly calculating which bone to break first.

The elevator dings. We're in a penthouse. His, if my research jibes with what I've seen of the interior. Walls of glass, city lights glittering like weapons outside, thrown back by the Hudson River. Clean modern furniture. Brutalist edges. Expensive, ill-gotten *everything*.

The burly men sporting terrifying bulges under their jackets drop me into a leather chair, tie me up again and leave.

He stays. Says nothing for a long time.

Just walks around me in a slow circle, the predator studying his prey. The silence is brutal. Designed to make me squirm.

I don't. But I want to.

I remind myself that I've dealt with a thousand variations of dark power and the evil it exudes.

Okay, so maybe not *this* level of concentrated power. The kind that urges me to celebrate my every breath because it may be my last.

He stops before me. Cants his head ever so fractionally.

Then he speaks again. Finally. "You've been very busy, little thief. Causing merry mayhem here, there and everywhere."

His voice is low, dark honey with a razored edge. It scrapes down my spine like the strike of a match, setting little fires everywhere.

I clench my jaw as those black eyes drill into mine. "Do you know how many times I watched you?"

Shit. I say nothing.

I'm hot defiance and righteous rage and I'm not shy about announcing it. Non-vocally. I've found in the past that works like a dream.

He leans in, voice just for me. "Since your very first heist.

The first time, you took down the Navarro family. I watched your livestream from my office. Thought it was a prank. By the third one, I started tracing your data. I knew your coding style. Sloppy in a charming way. Proud. Brash."

Fuck you.

He smirks. "By the fifth, I started to dream about you."

Umm. What? My skin prickles.

He crouches in front of me, eye level now. "Why do you do it, Specter?" His tone is curious, but his gaze never softens. "Or should that be Little Dahlia?"

I blink. Hard. My real name from his lips is like a slap. Sharp. Puncturing. It makes me almost forget the *little* part. That's the third... fourth time he's called me little. I'm keeping score on the size-baiting. And absolutely not thinking about him breaking me in half. Or about what else a man his size is packing. Nope nope *nope*.

"I see the way you rile up your followers. But I also sense your glee. So tell me, how much of this is a crusade?" he murmurs. "And how much is just rage you don't know where to put?"

I look away.

"No?" His voice lowers. "Is it because of Mommy?"

My heart stutters.

He doesn't know. He can't know. I made sure to scrub her from every last corner of the internet. "Fuck you."

That gets a smile. The devil, cracking open his box of toys. "Ah, she speaks. Hit a nerve, did I?"

I go cold. Silent. Exhale.

He circles again, slower this time. Deliberate.

"You wear your defiance like armor," he murmurs. "It's cute. But I wonder. What happens when I take that off? What do I find underneath?"

"You're not touching me," I spit.

He chuckles. Very much in a 'like you have a choice' way. "Not yet."

Not fucking ever. I brace. Cycle through every martial art technique I've learned, which is sadly a necessity for a woman like me.

He comes behind me, leans down—his breath a whisper against my ear. "You know what fascinates me?" he says softly. "You didn't ask where you are. Or why I've taken you. You didn't ask who I am or what I want."

His hand grazes the back of my chair. Not touching me. But close enough that I feel his heat. I hate what it's doing to my body. Because he's sharply observant, and it's only a matter of time before he sees my diamond-hard nipples. The pulse racing at my throat that's a fraction of panic and more... other things.

"You've already guessed. Because you're *smart*. Because you've seen me. And you know I'm not here to kill you. At least not yet."

I say nothing. Because he's right. Dante lives up to his name of bringing hell to those who wrong him. Slow. Excruciating. Hell. If the rumors bear out, this is just starting.

"You're scared," he whispers. "Not of me. Not really. You're scared I'll find what matters. Use it against you."

My stomach turns to ice.

He knows too much.

He *doesn't*, but he *does*.

"You left a trail," he murmurs. "Just a thread. A forgotten data tag on an old charity. A recurring transfer that breadcrumbs to a little house in Maine."

My heart kicks hard. He smiles like he hears it.

"A man living there. Older. Reclusive. Withdrawn. I wonder—would he survive a heart attack if the wrong people paid Dad a visit?"

I snap. "Don't you fucking touch him—"

Dante is in front of me in a flash, gripping the arms of the chair, caging me in with his body, his breath, his presence. So close I can feel heat roll off him in waves. Can smell the mint on his breath and the cold thunderstorm of his aftershave.

"Ah," he murmurs. "There it is. Your fire. Your weakness. Thank you, little thief. It's quite refreshing to see you're not masquerading as a boring wimp of a keyboard warrior. That should make this much more interesting."

He's not triumphant. He's not gloating. He's curious. Like he just cracked open a lockbox and is cataloguing the contents.

I shove back fear. Clench my fists. Shake my head like it might undo the moment. Erase what he's just threatened.

But he sees. He knows. "Don't worry," he says softly. "I won't hurt him. Not if you play nice."

I laugh, bitter and broken. "Is this the part where you break out the chains and call it justice?"

His smile goes dark. "Oh, Dahlia. You think I'm a monster? The devil even? Isn't that what the other D stands for?"

"Aren't you?"

He leans in close. "You stole from me. Seven-point nine mil in crypto. You livestreamed it. Mocked me. So yes, you're going to pay. One way or another."

"How? You're going to shatter every bone in my body? Dangle me from my toenails over your penthouse balcony?"

His features crack with the smallest of grimaces. "How unoriginal."

"What then? Because there's no fucking way you're getting your money back," I snap with far too much of that glee he mentioned. There are over six thousand people and thirty organizations out there tonight basking in Dante

O'Driscoll's unwilling largesse. I'll die before I take back even one cent of that.

"That's what insurance is for, little thief. By tomorrow night I'll barely have felt the loss of the money. But not the insult. That you will pay for. But I'm not interested in bruises. Not yet. I'm interested in surrender. Yours, so we're clear."

My breath catches.

He watches me. A cobra circling a mouse.

My vow not to speak lasts one revolution of my chair. "What does that mean?" I snap when he stops in front of me.

He doesn't hesitate. "It means I want thirty days."

"What?" My voice is barely there. "Thirty days of what?"

Hands shove into pockets. Eyes blacker than a wormhole. Mesmerizing. Coaxing me to my destruction. He waits a beat. Two.

"Thirty days of your life. Here. With me. You sleep in my bed. You wear what I give you. You obey my every demand. In return—you stay out of jail. Your father stays untouched. Safe. Oblivious to what his genius daughter has been up to. And," he breathes out, "you do one final heist. With me."

In my bed...

Heist...

In my bed.

Heist.

I swallow hard. Fight the stupid, giddy elation fizzling through my bloodstream.

This is madness. I absolutely should take my chances with calling his bluff, seeing what he does next. Probably torture. Definitely more threats. Would he be foolish enough to kill me when a few million followers know I planned to rob someone tonight?

I think not.

But... no one knows *who* I actually robbed. So Dante

O'Driscoll could disappear me and no one would be the wiser until it was way too late—

"Why?" I whisper, bypassing my own logic to satisfy the curiosity dancing beneath my skin.

He smiles. Cold and beautiful and lethal and terrifying. "Because you fascinate me, Dahlia. And because I want to know what it sounds like when you beg."

CHAPTER 4

Dahlia

I can't feel my hands anymore.

The restraints are cutting into my wrists, too tight, like he wants to make sure I remember who has the power.

But pain is easy. I can take pain. It's the *silence* that kills me.

He's just watching me, waiting for the answer I am absolutely not going to give.

From the shadows of his penthouse, Dante O'Driscoll leans back in an armchair like he's settling in to enjoy a show. One leg draped over the other. A tumbler of dark amber liquor in his hand. He hasn't touched it.

His eyes haven't left me.

I sit straight in the leather chair across from him, wrists tied to the arms, ankles bound beneath. Still dressed in my black gear, face smudged with dust and sweat. My hair's falling out of the wig I wore for the heist.

I must look feral. A street rat caught in a cage too golden to be real.

But I still have one weapon left.

My mouth. The silence thing was great while it lasted. Time to change things up.

"So what is this, Dante?" I say, injecting venom into his name. "Some twisted kink? You think if you tie me up and stare at me long enough, I'll melt into some grateful little sub and call you Daddy?"

He raises one brow. Sips.

Okay. A hit. Barely.

I keep going. "You're used to control. I get it. Mommy didn't hug you enough, and now you make your toys beg before you break them. Classic billionaire pathology."

His lips twitch. Fingers grip his glass just a fraction tighter.

Good. *Bleed, you bastard.*

"You think you've won. But you haven't," I spit. "You may have caught me, but I'll find a way out. There'll be people looking for me. I have a job."

"A minor obstacle, already taken care of."

"How?"

"The simple matter of buying the company you work for months ago. I'm your boss now. In all the ways you hope won't count."

Shocker. Also… what the fuck? I'm terrified to know how long he's been dangling this bait I've just deep-throated. "You're better off turning me over to the cops. Wash your hands of me and let's both forget tonight happened."

"And my money?"

I shrug. "Like you said. A drop in the ocean for guys like you."

"I also said something else, I'm sure."

The insult. Fuck.

"If you've been watching me, then you know I never divulge actual names before the heist. No one's the wiser."

"You know. I know," he parries softly. A poisoned caress.

When I manage to drag my gaze from him, I look around the room. A gilded cage. A silken prison. But it's me or Dad. "Seven days, no heist. I'm not helping you rob someone equally as despicable as you. Or worse, someone decent."

Sip. "Oh, they're much, much worse than me. But this isn't a negotiation, Little Dahlia."

Five.

The urge to swallow again overcomes me. I feel his gaze shift to my throat. Feel the heat of his eyes. Over me. *In me.* "Are you sure you want thirty days? I can give you thirty days of hell. And when I leave, I'll take your bank accounts, your offshore holdings, and maybe even your soul—if there's anything black enough left to sell."

He stands.

My mouth snaps shut. Instinct.

He moves slowly. No rush. That quiet, lethal grace that sets my nerves on fire.

He walks toward me, and every cell in my body screams to flinch. I don't.

He crouches in front of me again, gaze still burning through me.

Then, slowly… *that fucking smile*. Not cruel. Not mocking. *Knowing*. And fuck, why didn't I research deeper, arm myself with how fucking hot he is?

Because you never expected to encounter him.

"You done?" he asks.

My fists clench. I want to scream. I choose silence.

"I just want you to understand one thing," he murmurs. "You're not here because I *caught* you. You're here because I let you run long enough to show me who you really are. Perhaps even reward you if you live up to expectations."

My mouth goes dry.

He leans closer, until our faces are inches apart. "I watched you long before you ever typed my name into your righteous little poll. I let you choose me. I let you fantasize about punishing me. I let you want me."

I inhale sharply. "I never—"

"You did." He breathes it like scripture. "You wanted someone stronger than you. Smarter than you. Someone who'd take your control and shatter it so you could finally feel something that isn't rage or guilt or grief. That's what you've been searching for all this time. That's why you always head for the app when you're done. Because deep down, you're left unsatisfied."

I can't breathe.

"You went on The Club app for a reason, Dahlia. You didn't go looking for a boyfriend. You wanted to belong to someone—for just long enough to forget the burden of being the one who saves everyone."

My jaw clenches so hard it hurts. "You're projecting."

He brushes a lock of hair from my face, too gentle. "I'm revealing."

"No," I snap, voice cracking. "You don't know me."

"I know enough." He studies me. "Your mother died when you were sixteen. Truth-seeker. Idealist. She was your entire world. Your father collapsed after. You didn't. You turned your grief into a blade. You made it righteous. Purposeful."

No. No no no.

He leans in. "But when you wield a knife too tight you cut yourself too. You keep cutting without stopping to heal, Dahlia. You've just turned yourself into a martyr. And one day, it's going to destroy you." He stands again, looking down at me. "Unless someone stops you first."

There's a long silence.

My chest rises and falls too fast. I try to blink back the moisture burning behind my eyes. He can't see it. He *won't*.

He walks away to the bar. Refills his glass. Then turns back to me like none of that flaying ever happened.

"You have two choices," he says. "Thirty days. My rules. My bed. One job, together. When it's over, I'll erase your debt. You walk. No charges. Your father stays safe. Or…"

I look up. Brow arched.

"You disappear. Tonight. Permanently."

I laugh—shaky and hollow. "You think giving me a shit choice makes you merciful?"

"No," he replies calmly. "It makes me patient."

A beat. Two. "Patient," I echo.

"Because you'll never take option two. Because you might convince yourself that's what you'll do. But the hunger will keep gnawing at you until we're back here. With you tied to my chair. Still hungry. Still beautiful. Still craving me as much as I crave you."

I force my spine straight. Straighter. Because, holy shit, it wants to melt so bad and I don't recognize myself. Or maybe I do. Far too much. Because the next words out of my mouth are not what I mean to say. *Nope*.

And yet… "Fine," I say. "You want thirty days? You've got them."

He nods. Smug. Superior.

"But here's the thing, Dante," I add, voice like steel wrapped in silk.

"You think you're playing me. But I'm watching you, too. And by the end of this, when you break—I'll be the one collecting your pieces." His smile is slow, wolfish. "Ah, Dahlia," he murmurs. "Please make it worth my while and *try*."

CHAPTER 5

Dahlia

hree Weeks Ago

It's 3:43 AM.

The glow of my laptop screen is the only light in my tiny apartment in Brooklyn, half-covered by blackout curtains and the weight of too many secrets.

The heist is done. Clean. Fast. The money routed. Another corrupt asshole bankrupted. Another charity funded under a burner identity.

I should feel good. Triumphant. But I don't. I feel... empty. Wired. Angry and aching.

I tell myself it's adrenaline. That the crash will pass. But I know the truth.

I've been lying to myself for months.

Because the truth is: every time I take something from them, I want someone to take something from me.

The thought slips in uninvited.

I shouldn't feel this way. Not after everything I've achieved. Not after putting another monster down.

I close the tracking scripts. Then I hover over the icon I swore I'd delete—The Club.

Its sleek black logo pulses. Discreet. Dangerous. Invite-only. A digital dominion for people like them. The ones who want control. The ones who crave surrender.

I opened an account on a dare to myself. No photos. No name. Just a profile. Anonymous. Private. Safe.

Looking for something real.

That's what I wrote. Pathetic. But under the filters, the tags, the preferences... there was something more honest.

Submission.

Not the fake kind. Not roleplay. Not the watered-down power games everyone likes to pretend is enough.

I want the kind of surrender that *hurts*. That exposes. That strips me raw and makes me forget. *Makes me feel.*

Even if it terrifies me.

I scroll the message requests.

Dozens of them. Most I delete without reading. Too crass. Too boring. Too fake.

Then I pause.

New message. No name. Just a symbol. A chess knight.

I've been watching you.

You don't know what you're looking for. But I do.

When you're ready to stop pretending, come find me.

A three-second video of blood-red leather gloves, fingers linked. Resting on a dark surface. Waiting. For me.

My heart stutters. **Who are you?**

No response. I dig, because of course I do.

There's no profile attached. No contact info. No reply button. I check the back end. Nothing. It's clean. Too clean.

Someone built a fingerprint trap—snared my click, traced my pattern. Saw through the encryption.

I should be furious.

I should be scared.

But I'm wet.

And I don't even understand why.

CHAPTER 6

Dahlia

*P*resent Day

The restraints are gone.

I sit in a velvet chair near the tall windows of his bedroom, trying not to show how badly my legs are shaking.

The penthouse is quieter now. A little too still. I'm learning that Dante operates in stillness. Eerily so.

The walls are warm-toned steel and black stone, and everything about this room whispers dominance. No softness. No apologies.

And the bed—

God.

The bed is massive. Four posts and dark sheets. Heavy, masculine scent already coiled in the air like cologne and sin. A king's altar for every fantasy I never should've had. Never should've listed on The Club app on a stupid whim.

Dante emerges from the bathroom shirtless, suit pants swapped for expensive-looking lounge bottoms, toweling his hair. Sculpted. Fluid. Bronzed skin. Unfairly fucking beautiful. Like he was born from wrath and lust and filthy sin in equal measure.

He doesn't look at me as he speaks. "Take off your clothes."

I freeze. "What?"

He meets my eyes. Calm. Serious. "I want you naked when you get in my bed."

I want to throw something. Make demands. Plead for time. Instead, I stand—slowly. Like if I move too fast, I'll shatter with the force of the alien need moving through me.

He watches.

My fingers tremble as I strip. First the boots. Then the jacket. The clingy top. The cargo pants. Sports bra. My underwear last.

I stand there. Bare and burning. Hating myself for the tears stinging behind my eyes.

I shouldn't feel exposed. I've been naked with a guy before.

But not like this.

Never like this. Never with a man like him. One who sees so much. Too much. One who intends to lay me bare with scalpel-sharp purpose that will leave me bleeding and thankful.

Just like you wanted.

I ignore the insidious whisper as he walks to me slowly, eating the space between us.

Dark eyes coast over me, linger here and there but there's zero reaction to my naked body.

His hand lifts—and I flinch. But he only brushes a strand of hair behind my ear. "You're not a victim, Little Dahlia. You came looking for this."

The reminder, so close to that whisper, makes me want to slap him. Scream at him. Break his jaw. But my knees weaken instead. Floored by a truth I don't want to admit yet. Maybe never.

He takes my hand—warm touch, capable and powerful—and leads me to the bed. When I hesitate, he tugs me harder—like he's daring me to pretend I don't want it.

The sheets are soft. Cool. I lie down on my back. Heart slamming and nipples erect. Skin prickling with awareness.

He stands at the foot of the bed and watches, obsidian eyes glinting. Not so cold anymore. Then—he climbs in.

Over me. Caging me in.

His voice is a whisper at my ear. "I know what you crave. I read it between your lines the first night you logged on."

He brushes his fingers down my chest, ghosting over one breast, making me arch against my will. I shake my head.

He presses on, undaunted. "You want to give up control—but only to someone who can *truly* take it."

I try to turn my head. He captures my jaw, firm but not painful.

"You need someone stronger than your rage," he whispers. "Let me be that."

I don't answer. I can't.

But... sweet heaven... my legs fall open. Just slightly. Of their own damned volition. Betrayal and permission in one fucking little move.

And he smiles, like a king granted the keys to his favorite ruin.

He touches me. Just his fingers, slow and confident, dance down my body, leaving a trail of goosebumps and alarm in their wake. Almost clinically, they slide between my thighs. I gasp and try not to, but he hears it.

He keeps his eyes on mine the whole time.

"You'll learn," he says softly. "How to beg. How to break. And how it feels to be wanted... even when you're destroyed."

Up and down my slit. Stroke. Stroke. Stroke. But he doesn't push inside me. He doesn't take or conquer like I thought he would.

Instead—he withdraws.

And for a moment, I'm left wide open, bare and trembling, with need hanging in the air like a blade that never drops.

His hand glides upward, skimming my inner thigh, then my waist, mapping my body with the reverence of a man cataloguing an imperfect, priceless artifact—like he's searching for the exact point where I'll crack, and not a second too soon.

"You hide behind righteous fire," he murmurs, brushing the underside of my breast with the back of his fingers. "But I see the girl underneath. The one who hasn't been touched the right way. The one who wants someone to *know her* before they ruin her."

My nipples harden under the cool air and the hotter weight of his stare.

"I'm not some trembling virgin," I bite out, even though my voice betrays me. I'm not even sure why I uttered the V word. Because for all intents and purposes I am. Two fumbles at seventeen and twenty, brief and sticky and awful, don't experience make. And by protesting I sense I've just drawn attention to how inexperienced I truly am.

"No," he agrees, thumb grazing the tip of one breast, circling lazily until I have to clench my fists to stop from arching into him.

From breaking and begging as he so infuriatingly predicted. Because I'll be damned if I break in one night. *In one hour.*

"But you're inexperienced in the ways that matter. You've never let anyone *own* your pleasure."

I twist my face away.

He shifts—slow, deliberate, as if giving me time to acclimate to his intent, to *him*—and presses his mouth to my jaw.

Not a kiss. A test.

Then his lips drag down my neck. Behind my ear. Along my collarbone. Every press is soft, drugging, perfectly placed—designed not to claim, but to study.

By the time he kisses the center of my chest, I'm shaking, shocked, maddening words trembling on the tip of my tongue. How has he done this to me, *so fucking fast?*

He settles between my legs, half-clothed, propped on his elbows. I can feel the heat of his body, the steel pipe of his cock. Dear God, he can't be that big. The jagged edge of his restraint.

And still—he doesn't take.

He *hovers*. Watchful.

"Makes you crazy, doesn't it?" he says softly. "Not knowing when I'll give you what you want. Or if I will at all."

"I don't want anything from you," I hiss.

He smiles. "Liar. Hmm, maybe I should give you a nickname. Lying Little Dahlia."

Six. Seven?

His hand slides between my thighs again, cupping my pussy—bold, warm, steady, maddening. The pressure against my clit, my sopping center, is good. So fucking good. I moan before I can stop it.

His voice darkens. "I could make you come in under two minutes. No penetration. No toys. Just my hands. My mouth. My words."

I'm panting now. Humiliation and desire crash into each other, drowning everything else.

"But not tonight," he murmurs.

And just like that—his touch is gone. I'm left bare and buzzing, wet and stunned.

"No," I snap, tell myself I'm more angry with his stupid

stunts than with the loss of his touch and my thwarted hunger. "You don't get to play games—"

"I already did," he says, straightening, not even a little breathless. "And I won."

He looks down at me, the silk of his voice gone taut. "Sleep, Dahlia."

"I'm not a toy. I can't be switched on and off at your leisure. I can't fall asleep in a stranger's bed. I can't—"

"You can. You will." He brushes a thumb across my bottom lip. "Because I said so."

He steps back. Leaves me on the bed with every nerve screaming.

No more words. No satisfaction. No power.

Just… a burn. A hollow.

A *why did I want that? Why can't I stop wanting?*

He turns out the bedside light and disappears into the shadows of the room, then out the door, leaving me to lie there—aching, bewildered, furious.

And more afraid than I've ever been.

Not of him. Of myself.

And the worst part? I don't want to get up, get dressed, *explore my options*.

I don't want to run.

Because whatever game this is, I want to *win*.

CHAPTER 7

Dahlia

The sheets smell like him.

My first mistake is breathing too deeply. The scent is everywhere—spice and sin and something darker beneath it. I sit up fast, angry at myself for how my thighs clench from the memory alone.

No.

Last night was a game. A calculated push–pull. A mindfuck wrapped in silk sheets and whispered threats.

And I let him play me.

I swing my legs off the bed and pad across the warm marble floor to the huge glass windows. Manhattan stretches in every direction—morning light casting gold over steel and stone buildings and penthouses I've robbed or ruined.

Some of them even voted for their own downfall.

A bitter smirk curls my lips.

I glance around. No visible cameras, but I know better

than to believe I'm not being watched. *Always assume eyes.* It's rule number one in my playbook. Which makes my mistake last night even more painful to swallow. The fucking app.

I look around for my clothes but they're gone, whisked away by invisible hands while I slumbered in one of the most comfortable beds I've ever slept in.

Disgruntled by that, I find a robe draped over a nearby chair—soft, black, obviously his—snatch it up and wrap it around me. It drowns me and I hate how it smells like him too.

But it's better than nudity. Better than remembering how *naked and exposed* I felt beneath him.

With a deep breath I walk across the endless expanse of the bedroom and step out.

The penthouse is quiet. Too quiet. Until a door hisses open behind me. He steps out of some hidden corridor, already dressed in a tailored charcoal suit, cufflinks and watch glinting like weapons. He looks like a man who's conquered worlds before breakfast.

And he knows it.

"I want to talk about the heist," I say, sharp, level. I'm grasping, I know, hanging onto the only thing I can control. Because this man means to take away every other thing.

He walks past me, barely glances at me.

Down one corridor into another, then into a glass-walled terrace where breakfast is laid out. He stands beside one chair, his fingers tapping a beat.

Patient. Silent. *Fuck him.* Deadly as a gorgeous viper.

I want to test how long a standoff can last, but already a heavy pulse beats in my pussy. My nipples are hard points and fuck, he'll smell my arousal if my thighs keep clenching and unclenching like a blacksmith's bellows.

I step forward and take the seat, wondering if his lips just ghosted over my temple or I imagined it.

When I glance over he's sitting down, pouring espresso from a silver carafe. "There's time for that."

"No, there's not. Thirty days means little if I don't know what this is about. I want details. Timing. Target. Access points."

He hands me a second cup, like this is just a normal Tuesday morning and not the aftermath of high-stakes seduction warfare.

I don't take it.

He sets it down on the counter between us anyway. "Drink. You'll need the caffeine."

"Stop pretending this is normal."

"Why not?" His gaze lifts to mine—calm, unreadable. "You've fantasized about this. Shall I recite your naughty little cravings?"

My breath catches.

He leans closer. Not touching. Just close enough to crowd me.

"You play the rebel well, little thief. But you want structure. Boundaries. A leash." His voice lowers, velvety and dangerous. "And you want me to hold it."

"Fuck you," I whisper.

He smiles. Smug and patient. "You will."

I spin away, hands shaking, furious at myself for how hot my skin feels.

"How many others?" I demand. "How many women have you done this to? Clearly if you used The Club app then you're on there too." What the hell is that sensation in my diaphragm? Because it sure as fuck isn't jealousy!

His pause is deliberate. The glimmer in his eyes, searing. "None like you."

The words hit harder than they should. I shouldn't care.

But I *do*.

Because I don't know what game he's playing anymore—and worse, I don't know if I'm still playing too.

* * *

Dante

SHE THINKS she still has a chance of getting out of this.

The way she stood this morning—bare feet braced like she was ready to launch herself at me, eyes full of fire and teeth bared beneath a thin sheen of control—she was magnificent. Terrified. Gorgeous.

And still foolish enough to think this is a game she can win.

That robe she wore? Mine. That espresso she wouldn't take? Mine. The building? The city view? The *air*?

All. Mine.

But the delicious part is that she hasn't realized yet: I'm not her captor.

I'm her *mirror*. I will dominate. She will submit.

And I've already won. Not because I broke her. Because I'm going to teach her how to want to be broken.

That's the difference.

God, she's sexy when she fights. When she tries to negotiate with a blade tucked behind her words, like she hasn't already handed me every weapon I need.

She doesn't know it yet, but the real heist started the moment she created that Club profile. That soft confession buried under bravado.

Looking for something real.

Not money. Not sex. *Powerlessness*, freely given. Craved.

I know what she needs. Because I hacked her preferences,

mapped her clicks, read between the lines of every vanilla rejection she swiped left.

I built her cage perfectly.

Thirty days is generous. I could break her in half that time.

But I want it slow. I want her *aware*. I want her to *choose* the fall. Because when she finally surrenders, it won't be desperation.

It'll be *devotion*.

I'll peel her open with words, touches, the kind of pleasure that rewires a woman's soul. And she'll beg—*beautifully*. Because she's never been worshipped properly.

She's been surviving. Hustling. Clawing her way through a world built to swallow girls like her.

But Dahlia Wynn doesn't understand how rare she is. How exquisitely, dangerously rare. Not just because of her tech skills—which, admittedly, are sharp enough to make her a threat—but because she doesn't hesitate to get her hands dirty. She walks into the lion's den live-streaming herself, wearing her sins and defiance like sequins.

She wants to be seen, even as she hides.

Most hackers, even the best, stay shadows. Ghosts. Digital tricksters behind encrypted walls.

Not her.

My little thief thrives on impact. On justice and judgment.

And now she's mine.

In the very building she tried to stage her little Robin Hood stand last night, I lean back in my chair, scrolling through the feed she thinks I haven't found. Her alias account. The poll. The comments.

Her followers are rabid for blood. They eat up her moral grandstanding. Vote on targets like it's a marginally less bloody Squid Game. Most of them don't realize she's actually doing it. The rest? Fanatics.

It would be easy to take her down.

But unfortunately, I need her. Not just for the spectacle and the sublime promise of her surrender I got a taste of last night, but for the *access*.

She's the key to something locked up tighter than anything I can buy or bribe my way into. Not because she's smarter—but because no one's looking at her. Because the target she doesn't know I've chosen has been planning this longer than she's been alive.

And there's a window opening soon—just one shot to reclaim what was stolen from me years ago.

And I need *her* to get it.

I could've forced her. Threatened her father some more. Broken her in the usual ways. But that wouldn't have ultimately worked.

Because she doesn't fear pain and I don't want her furious or anxious. She fears exactly what she needs—relinquishing her *power*.

Which is why I'll give her the illusion of control. Let her crawl back toward agency… while I take her apart cell by cell. And when she gets what I need—when she hands me the prize, bleeding from the inside out—I'll reward her the only way she truly wants.

With her unsullied surrender.

My cock jumps in my pants. Furious. Ready.

Dahlia. At my feet. It's almost too heady to contain. But contain it I will.

Thirty days. And maybe then… *maybe*… I'll let her go.

Or… not? Fuck, even I don't believe that anymore. But I know under all that rage, she wants to be seen.

Owned.

Kept.

And maybe I will keep her.

I watch her prowl from room to room in my penthouse, bouncing on the balls of her feet. Silent, sexy as the sweetest Belladonna. One I wanted to consume, wholeheartedly and fatally last night. In all my years as a Dominant I've never come close to calling *fuck it* and fucking a woman without proper, basic ground rules, the way I did last night. I grip the erection that hasn't subsided since I cornered her in this building twelve hours ago.

Exhale. Inhale. Exhale.

I didn't expect it to feel like this. Like addiction. Like *purpose*. Like she's not just a tool to use against my enemies.

She's a match, flickering under everything I've kept cold for so long.

And something about the way she looked at me—shaking and furious and still wanting—hit deeper than it should have.

I need her for the plan.

But God help me…

I think I want Dahlia for a whole lot more.

CHAPTER 8

Dahlia

I hear the elevator hum before I see him.

All day I've been pacing this penthouse like a caged animal. No phone. No laptop. No tools. Just the sound of my own anxiety echoing back at me from polished marble floors and glass walls.

He's *planned this*. That's the part that stings. That makes the fight in my chest burn hotter. Because if Dante O'Driscoll has planned this, it means he's known who I am for longer than I realized. And I hate being outmaneuvered.

There's a room in this glass palace that I hadn't dared return to after one glimpse this morning. A closet—or rather, a *boutique*. My measurements. My style. My name scrawled in delicate gold foil on boxes I didn't ask for. Lingerie so delicate it might vanish if you breathed too hard. Dresses that slide like sin over skin.

And in the corner, a desk. With a brand-new laptop locked in a case I couldn't crack without explosives.

The temptation mocked me all day. But what really fucked with me? The message taped to the screen in Dante's perfect handwriting.

Earn this.

I'm still burning from it when he steps into the marble-floored foyer. And adding to the pile of things I hate? I can't stop myself from devouring him.

Dark suit. Dark shirt. No tie. Coat slung over one mile-wide-linebacker shoulder. Black hair tousled from wind and probably some high-powered criminal meeting with people on my shit list.

He looks at me like I'm already on my knees. I stand taller because fuck that.

"Pacing suits you," he murmurs. "Like a lioness in heat."

"Screw you," I snap even while flames dance beneath my skin because he's confirmed there are cameras in here. And he's been watching me.

He smiles. *Fuck*, I hate when he does that.

"Strip," he says casually, walking past me into the living room.

My breath catches, my pussy melts and my nipples sting. "What?"

"You heard me." He sets down his keys, loosens his cuffs. "Clothes off. All of them."

I cross my arms. "No."

He turns to face me. Not angry. Not threatening. Just *expectant*. "This isn't about sex, Dahlia," he says softly. "It's about trust."

I laugh, bitter. "Trust? Why the fuck should I trust you? You kidnapped me."

"And yet here you are. Waiting. Watching the door." His

gaze drops to my feet then trails back up, leaving a path of fire. "Wet."

Heat floods my cheeks. "I am not—"

"You're not stupid. So don't act like you don't know what's happening here."

I hate how calm he is. How measured. Like I'm already halfway into his palm and we're just negotiating the speed of my fall.

"I want to show you something," he says. "But I won't touch you unless you follow the rules." His eyes return to my feet again, bare because when my clothes were miraculously returned my boots weren't.

He seems... fascinated by them.

Does Dante O'Driscoll have a foot fetish?

Gah, I don't want to know. "What rules?"

"The rules I'm about to give you."

He walks over to me slowly. Doesn't touch. Just stands close enough that I feel the heat of his body like a current under my skin.

"Strip, Dahlia," he murmurs. "That's rule number one."

My breath trembles. I should say no. But my fingers are already moving.

Belt. Cargo pants. Turtleneck. I pause. He waits, not even an eyebrow raised.

I swallow. Bra. Panties. Each piece makes my skin feel thinner. By the time I'm naked, I'm fighting tremors and the urge to clench my thighs.

He walks behind me. I feel his breath at my neck. A little faster, hotter than normal.

"Hair down," he instructs. And his voice is hoarser too.

Dante isn't as unaffected as he projects. I revel in the tiny punch of power even as I raise my hands and obey his instruction. The weight of my long hair caresses my skin, expanding every shiver of awareness. Making my breath shorten more.

"You're going to kneel now. Not because I forced you. Because you choose to." His voice darkens, low and dangerous. "Because you want to know what it's like to be handled properly."

I hesitate.

Every stubborn cell in my body screams at me to defy him. To smirk. To spit some smart, bitter line about consent or autonomy or how men like him always think they're in control. But none of it makes it to my lips.

Because something *else* is stirring.

A pressure beneath my skin, heavy and undeniable. It's not fear. Not even lust. It's gravity. Like I've been resisting the pull of something for so long that I forgot what surrender feels like—and now, standing here, stripped down to nothing but nerve and instinct, I feel it pressing into my bones. A strange, aching need to let go, just enough to see what happens when someone else takes the reins.

I sink to my knees.

Quietly. Without drama.

Without any show of reluctance—because that would be a lie. The marble is cold against my skin, but that's not what makes me tremble.   It's the silence that follows.

The slow, deliberate way he breathes as he looks down at me. As if he's known all along that I'd do it. That part of me wanted this—*craved* this. And I hate that he might be right. I hate it so much... it almost makes me wet.

Nah, forget *almost*.

Dante walks in front of me, crouches to my level. "Look at me."

I do.

"This isn't about you giving up control," he says. "It's

about learning where it feels best to let go. You fight everything. Everyone. But I know you, Little Dahlia. I know what you need."

My breath hitches. "You don't know shit."

He smiles again, and it's *dangerous*.

"Rule number two," he says. "You will speak when spoken to. Ask permission to come. And always tell me the truth."

Fat chance. But my jaw clenches, halts my protest. He hasn't given me permission yet.

He reaches out—slowly—and runs his knuckle down the center of my chest. Not quite touching my nipple. Just close enough to make me ache. To make me move towards him. Make me hate him a little for it.

"Do you understand?"

My mouth is dry. It shouldn't be able to form the word. Yet… "Yes."

He leans in, lips grazing my ear.

"Good girl. Rule three. You belong to me during your training. Your pussy. Your clit. Your pleasure. The air you breathe. All mine. And I'll use it or deny it as I see fit."

My thighs clench involuntarily. "I haven't agreed to anything," I whisper.

"No," he says. "But your body has."

His hand slides between my thighs—barely a brush—and I flinch. "Already wet for me," he croons. "And I haven't even touched your pretty little clit."

His fingers hover. So close. So maddening. Then—one perfect stroke.

My head falls back. A moan tears out of me before I can stop it. But just as fast, his hand disappears. I choke on a protest.

He leans down, lips brushing my jaw. "That's your first lesson. Remember, you don't come unless I let you."

I'm kneeling. Naked. Breathless. *Furious.*

And desperate for more.

"Up," he says as he stands, adjusting his cuff. A tiny flex of sophistication totally undermined by the savage hunger pulsing from him. By the fat steel rod pushing against his fly.

I obey before I can stop myself.

He takes something from his pocket. Slim. Leather. Expensive. Gold clasp.

A collar.

"No," I breathe, pulse leaping. "Fuck no."

"This isn't a leash," he says patiently. Far too fucking patiently. "It's a promise."

He holds it up, one inch from my nose. For an eternity. Then, whatever he sees in my face, he nods and steps behind me. "Say the words, Dahlia."

A promise. Of what? Why does every cell in my body want to know? Why is the three-letter word shivering to be on my tongue, crowding, crowding, crowding, *desperate* to get out?

Thirty days... well, twenty-nine now.

I sincerely doubt Dante intends to let me out of this penthouse. He planned this meticulously, knew no one would miss me publicly because my laptop is my office. Dad will lose track of time until I contact him, remind him I exist.

I lick my lips. Rationalize.

If no one sees me in it, then surely it's fine, right? This breaking and wanting and surrendering and collaring will only be between us. Our little filthy secret.

"Yes." The word falls out before I can stop it.

Still, he waits. My jaw clenches, but again, it's not enough to uproot my next response from my soul.

"Yes, Sir," I breathe.

"Good girl," he murmurs again. Then he fastens it around my neck. Not tight. Just *present*.

He steps closer, wrapping his power, his aura around me.

"You belong to me now, Dahlia. And when I say kneel, you'll kneel. When I say come, you'll come."

He steps in front of me again. Brushes a knuckle down my sternum.

He tilts my chin up.

Then Dante's mouth crashes into mine—hot and hard and *everything*.

A promise and a punishment all at once, and I don't have time to think—I only *feel*. The heat of it. The hunger. The way his hand fists in my hair, dragging me closer, angling my face so he can take exactly what he wants, how he wants it.

He's fully clothed and I'm a naked accessory for his pleasure.

And holy shit, why does that light me the fuck up?

His lips are firm, commanding, coaxing mine open with a flick of his tongue, and the second I let him in, I know I've made a mistake. Because it's not just a kiss. It's an invasion. A seduction. A *branding*.

It's him mapping every inch of my mouth like he already owns it. He tastes like sin—dark and expensive, whiskey-laced and wicked—and he kisses like he wants to ruin me from the inside out.

My body betrays me instantly, heat sparking low in my belly, knees going soft as my fingers curl into his shirt without permission.

I tell myself I hate it. That I hate *him*. That this is a game and I'm just playing my part—but the lie rings hollow when I realize I'm kissing him back with just as much hunger. Maybe more. Because his kiss feels like everything I've ever denied myself. The absence of control. Craving. Safety wrapped in danger.

And God help me, I want more. I *need* more.

Even as my pride screams at me to pull away, to slap him, to do anything but moan into his mouth the way I do now, I stay pressed against him like he's the only solid thing in a world that's always shifting beneath my feet.

By the time he pulls away, my knees are weak.

He grips my waist, thumbs stroking my pelvic bone, back and forth, back and forth. Then he whispers against my lips. "Go to bed, Dahlia."

I stare at him, stunned. "Are you serious? You're leaving me like this?"

"Of course," he says, voice low and full of dark promise. "Obedience starts with *denial*."

He turns. Walks away.

And leaves me there—collared, wet, empty…

And… terrifyingly… already halfway his.

* * *

IN A DAZE I watch the door click shut behind him.

The moment I'm alone, my knees go weak for real. I don't collapse—but it's close. I scrabble up my clothes and hightail it to the bedroom I used last night.

My skin feels too sensitive to put them back so I dump them on the bed and shrug into the robe I used this morning.

My shaking hand rises to my neck. The collar is still snug around my neck. Light. Elegant. Mocking. I finger the clasp, already knowing bone deep that I'm going to leave it on.

My body is still trembling. From his touch. His voice. His kiss. His *restraint*.

God, I hate him. I hate that I can't stop thinking about how close his fingers were to my pussy. How easily he denied me. How much I *wanted* to obey.

But hate is sharp. Useful. It gives me just enough clarity to focus on what really matters: Escape.

Or if not *escape*… leverage.

I move back to the door, stop, listen. Then I step back out

into the hallway and walk through the penthouse with a purpose. Barefoot. Silent.

He thinks I'll go to bed like an obedient pet.

Newsflash, I'm a *fucking thief*.

I return to the room and head straight for the desk. The laptop case is still there. Untouched.

A keycard opens it. Not a password. That was the first layer. I figured that out this morning. But now I see the second: a fingerprint reader.

And a tiny port at the back for an external interface.

Amateur hour, O'Driscoll.

I take out the hairpin I grabbed from the vanity in the room I suspect he made up for me. Use the spiral to trigger the latch on the case. It clicks open.

The screen lights up. A security prompt flashes.

Welcome back, D.

My lips curl. Cocky bastard.

I bypass the start screen with a cloned instance of his OS—a mirrored shadow shell I planted during my last heist. I only had a few seconds of proximity, but I got enough metadata to exploit. Enough to trick the machine into thinking I'm him—for five minutes max.

My hands fly over the keys.

Folder after folder. Financials. Blackmail. Offshore accounts.

One file named "Ironveil: Access Protocol."

Another flagged "Wraith." Encrypted.

That second name makes my stomach twist. It was my codename once.

From another life.

From before my mother died.

Before I started calling myself Specter.

Before I decided I'd rather hunt monsters than grieve like a good daughter.

Coincidence? Maybe.

I don't breathe as my fingers hover, hesitating—but the urge to know is louder than the instinct to stay safe. Fuck it.

The screen flashes **RED**.

ALERT.

Unauthorized Access Detected.

Lockout Sequence Initiated.

Unsurprising but still... *shit*. The desk hums beneath my palm.

And then the collar around my throat vibrates. A single pulse.

What the hell?

My fingers fly to my neck, memories of some Z-movie character dying with a collar-shock freewheeling through my mind.

Surely he's not that crass. That inelegant. Because that would be... disappointing.

The gold clasp warms—just slightly. Not painful. Not yet. Just a warning. A reminder.

And then a message appears on screen:

Disobedience earns punishment, little thief.

Go to the playroom.

Kneel.

Wait.

I freeze. My heart starts to hammer like it's trying to escape. He knew I'd try. He left this here like bait. Like a fucking test. Again. And I walked right into it.

The collar cools. My skin still tingles with shame. With something darker.

Now I have a choice.

Run? Try to hack my way out of the penthouse altogether, take my chances with the cops? With death?

Or... obey?

God help me—I stand, walk out, head to the other room I

discovered in my fury tour today. The room with more toys and gadgets than The Club app that landed me in this shit in the first place.

I walk to the center of the room.

And I kneel on the leather mat reserved for my shame.

In the room he built just for this.

CHAPTER 9

Dante

One Hour Later

SHE KNEELS EXACTLY where I expected her to.

Not looking up. Naked again.

Her hair is wild and hands loose. Thighs trembling. Mouth set in that stubborn pout I already dream about ruining.

I walk around her once. Twice.

She stays still. Breathtaking. A good girl when she wants to be. "You broke the rule," I say quietly.

She lifts her chin but keeps her eyes downcast. "So punish me." A hint of a brat in there. She's cute, my chaos-baiting thief.

I smile, feeling the fire of her gaze even without looking into her eyes.

"No."

She blinks. "What?"

"You want punishment. That's too easy. You want the guilt. The burn. The righteous pain." I stop in front of her. Tilt her face up and yep, blue lightning, gorgeous and deadly. "But what you *don't* know yet is how devastating mercy can be."

Her breath shudders and for a moment, she looks utterly panic-stricken. Confused. My gut clenches. I release it with a breath.

Release her, pace back to sit in the armchair across from her. Unfasten my belt and whip it free. Leave it draped on my thigh—just a threat. "Do you crave some relief, Little Dahlia?"

On cue, her eyes blaze. She thinks I haven't noticed how that adjective riles her. How not-so-silently she plots retribution for the slight.

Anticipation simmers, alien and delicious. When was the last time I craved like this? Felt this transcendental calling?

Never.

But she's good—if not great—at compartmentalizing. Or her hunger is greater. Either way, my question concentrates her. Her eyes return to the belt. A tremor seizes me. How I wish I could test the edges of her pain but not tonight. Not this soon. I haven't even tested a single limit yet.

"Answer me, Dahlia. It's not a trick question."

Her nostrils quiver. "So what if I do? Your baiting is getting old."

"The words you want, are 'yes please, sir' or 'no, thank you, sir.'"

Mutiny reigns, bright and beautiful. Then her thighs

tremble again. Her chin drops a fraction and she exhales. "Yes. Sir."

"Good girl. For that, I'm going to let you touch yourself tonight," I say softly. "But only under one condition."

She narrows her eyes. "Which is?"

"You don't come unless I say. If you do, I'll lock you in this room. Deny you for *days*."

Her cheeks flush. Her thighs squeeze. She's so wet I can see the shimmer of her slick pussy from here. Smell her beautiful musk.

My cock fills, throbs, as hunger rips a wider chasm within me.

"I won't beg," she whispers.

"You already have," I murmur. "But not with words." I motion with my hand. "Lie back. Open wide. Show me."

She hesitates. Then obeys.

"Wider. I know how flexible you are, my pretty little cat burglar. I've watched you get in and out of some impressively tight spaces."

"How?"

He smiles. "Do what I ask and I'll tell you."

She eases back completely on the soft leather mat on the floor. Legs spread. Face flushing with self-consciousness, yes. But also with arousal. She's been on edge since last night. I'm mildly stunned she didn't attempt to alleviate it in between attempting to hack into every electronic device she could find in the apartment.

Slowly, one arm rises to rest above her head, unpractised and natural, the other already sliding down to her slit.

"Stop."

A mingled whine and angry protest. But she waits.

"Say it," I order. "Say who owns your pussy. Your pleasure. And look at me when you do."

She swallows. Squeezes her eyes shut for a moment. Then. "You do."

I raise an eyebrow. "Say it *right*."

Her voice is barely more than a whisper. "You own my pussy, Dante. And my pleasure."

"Not quite there yet." I murmur, ignoring the pain pulsing through my balls. I've never been this heavy. This fucking ravenous in my life. I'll need to take care of it tonight or I'll be useless tomorrow.

"You own my pussy and my pleasure, Sir," she breathes. Her fingers quiver against her neatly trimmed mons.

"Good girl. Now… play."

"Tell me how first, Sir."

I curb another smile. Even horny and desperate, she craves knowledge. "I hacked your trusty little drones. Every time you turned them on, I got a ringside view."

A wince. Disappointment in herself. "Fuck."

Her fingers flick with irritation.

"I hope you're not going to take out your temper tantrum on my pussy, Dahlia," I warn softly. "Because there will be punishment for that. One I guarantee you won't like."

She stops a whisper away from her labia. Breathes in. Out. In. Then she tries again. Light circles at first. She gasps at her own touch.

It's beautiful.

Raw.

And I don't say a word. Not for long minutes. Not while she writhes and bites her lip and chokes back moans.

I let her build close. So *close*.

Until her hips buck and her breath gets ragged. Until her clit puffs up, full and eager.

"Stop."

She whimpers. Freezes.

I rise and walk over. Kneel beside her. Slide two fingers between her thighs and find her clit.

Just one stroke. She jerks.

"No," I murmur. "Not yet."

Her body's *screaming* for it. But her eyes? They're wild with need.

"I want to come," she whispers. "Please."

My cock throbs. Still, I wait. Drag my fingers alongside her clit but not quite touching it. Teasing. Edging. Her nipples are sharp points that beg for my lips. For the punishing twists of my fingers. So fucking beautiful.

Her eyes flutter shut. "Please." Her voice breaks.

"You may come," I say softly. "But only if you thank me for denying you."

"Thank you for making me wait, Sir," she gasps. "Thank you for… owning me."

"Claim your reward, baby. Come for me."

A harsh cry and her body breaks apart under my fingers —desperate, keening, *ruined*.

I sip and lick at her lips as she flails beautifully on my mat, her pussy clenching, clenching, growing wetter with my strokes. Drenching me. Saturating me in my own need.

The urge to free my cock, sink in and ride the coattails of her climax is beyond overwhelming. Even the temporary high of licking her cum off my fingers feels like a breaking point.

So I tug my hanky from my pocket. Wipe it off. Then I kiss her throat.

And whisper: "Tomorrow, you'll start earning your way out."

* * *

Dahlia

. . .

Dante doesn't let me sleep in.

He wakes me before dawn with a command in my collar —turns out it's electronic, the bastard—and a single word vibrating through the device like silk-wrapped steel.

"**Up.**"

I jerk awake, disoriented and aching in places I shouldn't be.

By the time I stumble out of bed and find the oversized walk-in closet, he's already laid out what I'm supposed to wear.

Black pants. Slim, tight. A sleeveless blouse in sheer ivory silk with nothing to hide under it. No bra. No underwear. Just my skin and the cool air and the weight of his gaze when I step into the main room, trying not to cross my arms over my chest like a self-conscious coward.

He doesn't comment.

But his jaw tightens. His eyes drop to my nipples, hard and visible through the fabric, and something *hungry and savage* glints in his gaze before it disappears behind that smooth, terrifying composure.

"This is day one," he says. "Today, you learn how we work."

We.

It's the first time he's spoken as if I'm not just a possession. As if I might *matter* to his goals.

But I don't let myself feel anything like pride. Not with the way he stares at me. Not with the way he taps the tablet in his hand and displays the blueprint of the building we'll be targeting. Rathe Tower. Obsidian Corp's crown jewel.

"A test run on my building. You'll get limited access," he says. "Enough to set up the electronic scaffolding. No direct taps yet. No extraction. I want to see how you move. How you improvise."

"And if I don't play nice?"

He looks up, slow and deliberate, charcoal-gray eyes burning with something cold and deadly. "Then I teach you obedience. Again."

My body flares with a memory—his fingers, his voice, the wicked precision of his denial. I flush. He sees it. *Of course* he sees it.

His mouth curves, and then he nods toward the worktable. "Start here. Crack the gatekeeper protocol."

I lean in. "Blind? No salt strings? No decoys?"

He tilts his head. "Did I stutter, Specter?"

Heat licks my spine. I want to fly at him, rip him apart with nails and words, but it's been over a day since I was properly online, and dammit, I've got withdrawal symptoms in the worst way. And I have a feeling he knows *that* too.

I move to the terminal, hands already dancing over keys, diving deep into encrypted net-structures. And I feel it the moment I brush the ghost of a backdoor—custom coded, tangled in his fingerprints.

He *wants* me to see it. Just enough to bait me.

My jaw clenches. I don't take the bait.

Yet.

* * *

OVER THE NEXT THREE DAYS, Dante pushes me hard.

There's no rhythm, no comfort zone. One minute, we're side by side parsing security strings and brute-forcing obsolete defenses.

The next, he's dragging me into the playroom for lessons I don't even realize I'm failing until I'm gagged, wrists bound behind me, pulse hammering as he whispers, "You broke posture again. That's ten minutes kneeling, no speaking, hands on your thighs. Eyes down. Learn your place."

I *hate* how fast I learn it.

But I hate even more how my body loves it.

He never fucks me. But his hands… God. They're everywhere.

Rough and soft.

Demanding and patient.

Exploring and *withholding* until I ache in ways I don't have names for. He teaches me the freedom to strip on command without protest.

How to ask—properly—before touching myself.

"You'll earn every goddamn stroke," he growls one night, his mouth inches from my cunt as I tremble, sweat-slicked and leaking onto silk sheets I've stained with my shame.

"Please," I gasp. "Dante—please—"

And I hate myself for how much I enjoy the taste of my own begging.

* * *

THE FOURTH NIGHT begins like the others: with silence.

But tonight, the silence is heavier, charged with anticipation.

Dante stands by the edge of the bed, his charcoal-gray eyes fixed on me. His gaze is intense, unwavering, as if he's trying to read every thought that crosses my mind.

"Strip," he commands, his voice low and firm.

I obey, my fingers trembling slightly as I remove each piece of clothing. The air is cool against my skin, causing goosebumps to rise. Standing naked before him, I feel both vulnerable and empowered.

He approaches, holding a small, sleek toy in his hand. I

BAD GIRL DILEMMA

know what it is. An anal plug. It's surprisingly pretty for something I know for sure is going to hurt.

"Tonight, we add a new element," he says, his tone devoid of emotion, yet his eyes betray a flicker of something deeper.

I nod, recalling the list of limits I filled out days ago. This was within the boundaries I set, and when it comes to this, to surrendering, he's in charge. And while I can't say I trust him farther than I can throw him, for now, my surrender serves us both.

He guides me to the bed, positioning me on all fours. His hands are steady, thoughtful, even a touch indulgent. He stares at me for an age, a slow sizzle in his eyes that tells me he likes what he sees. Well, if he doesn't then he needs to have a word with that hot rod in his pants.

I'm caught in a half-laugh, half-terror situation that luckily stays trapped inside as Dante prepares me. A trail of kisses on my neck, shoulders, down my spine.

A generous smearing of lube on the plug.

Then an unfamiliar sensation, a mix of discomfort and curiosity.

His fingers glide between my butt cheeks and oh God, that's so alien but... interestingly sensual. No, fuck sensual. I'm getting wet. Dripping. Tensing as heat turns into a hot little blaze low in my belly.

"Relax. Breathe," he instructs, his voice softer now. He steps closer, his eyes ravenously devouring my every expression. "Look at me, Dahlia."

I look up into his furnace-hot face and whatever he sees in mine makes his cock surge, once, behind his fly. Drags color high into his sculpted cheekbones.

"You're ready." It's an edict. Inescapable.

I nod and inhale deeply, focusing on the rhythm of my breath, feel him place the tip of the toy against my puckered hole and force myself not to tense.

Slowly, he inserts the plug, pausing at intervals to ensure I'm comfortable. Once it's fully in place, he gently caresses my lower back, a silent gesture of reassurance.

"Good girl," he murmurs, and a shiver runs down my spine, far too thrilled with the praise.

He helps me to my feet, guiding me to stand before him. His eyes roam over my body, taking in every curve, every detail. He circles me once, his fingers brushing over the broad jeweled base of the plug. I clench around it and God, it's... terrifyingly incredible.

"You're beautiful," he says, his voice thick with emotion.

I look up at him, meeting his gaze. "Thank you," I whisper, my voice barely audible.

He leans in, his lips brushing against mine in a tender kiss. It's soft, exploratory, a stark contrast to the intensity of our previous encounters.

As the kiss deepens, I feel a warmth spread through me, a connection forming that's more than just physical.

He pulls back slightly, resting his forehead against mine. "Remember, if at any point you want to stop, use your safe word," he reminds me.

"I remember," I reply, appreciating his constant emphasis on consent.   He leads me to the bed, positioning me on my back. His hands explore my body, tracing patterns that ignite every nerve ending. The plug adds a new layer of sensation, intensifying every touch.

He teases me, bringing me to the brink of release before pulling back, a wicked smile playing on his lips.

"Please," I beg in a voice laced with desperation.

"Not yet," he replies, his tone teasing.

He continues this dance, pushing me to the edge repeatedly, each time leaving me more desperate than before.

Finally, he leans in, his mouth inches from my core. His tongue flicks out, delivering a single, tantalizing lick.

I gasp and arch towards him, seeking more but he pulls back, his breath ragged. His hands grip the edge of the mattress, shoulders tense.

"You're testing my control." His voice is ragged and strained.

I reach out, placing a hand on his cheek. "Then let go," I whisper.

He hesitates, the internal battle evident in his eyes. But after a moment, he leans in, capturing my lips in a passionate kiss.

His tongue flicks once. Just once.

I nearly come undone.

But he pulls away again, breath once again ragged. And in that split second, I see the deeper crack.

He's unraveling too.

His jaw is tight with restraint, like he's one more moan away from doing exactly what he swore he wouldn't: burying himself inside me and losing control.

He doesn't. He leaves me wrecked and desperate.

Again.

But every night, he stays longer.

And every time he leaves, he looks back like he's not sure if walking away is strength... or useless denial.

* * *

DANTE'S CONTROL has been absolute since the moment I woke up in his world.

His rules, his voice, his collar. Every lesson was a calculated domination. And for a while, I let it happen. Not because I was broken. But because I was *learning*.

Mapping him the same way I map firewalls—slowly, carefully, until I find the crack.

Today, I find it.

We're in the training room, blueprints and security layers projected across the wall, Dante pacing behind me like a dark predator. His instructions are crisp. Authoritative and clinical. But I'm no longer distracted by his voice or the heat of his gaze.

I'm watching his hands. The subtle twitch of his jaw when I reroute a protocol before he finishes describing it.

"I said we'd come at it from the west perimeter," he says, his tone low, edged with warning.

"And that would be smart," I reply, not looking up. "If we wanted to trigger every tripwire embedded since 2020. But I found an unpatched exploit in their archival vault from the south conduit. Quiet. Efficient. And invisible—unless you're actually looking."

Silence stretches behind me.

I finally glance over my shoulder.

He's staring at me, his black gaze unreadable. The screen's glow catches the gold at his throat and the faint scar that traces the line of his collarbone.

God, he's beautiful. Dangerous. Deadly, even. But fuck, I want to cut myself on all his edges and bleed out my needs.

Right now, though, I catch something else.

And for the first time he looks... *uncertain*.

"You disapprove of my correction, Mr. O'Driscoll?" I say, and I know how mocking I sound, but I don't stop. Because if he's the king of cold control, I'm the queen of exploiting cracks. It's what's earned me my name, respect and a nice, fat bank balance.

He tilts his head slightly. "Are you disobeying me, Specter?"

That name. On his lips. A warning. A stroke right between my legs. God. "I'm *disputing* you. There's a difference. I might be your submissive in the bedroom but you're my partner in this. Not your puppet."

He doesn't speak. That alone is a victory.

I rise from my seat slowly, turning to face him fully. The tension is a live wire between us. I feel it in the quickening of my pulse, in the way his eyes drop—just for a fraction of a second—to my mouth before dragging back up. That too is *new*.

He's always touched me with brutal intent but never looked at me like I *might* have teeth too.

I take a step forward. He doesn't move.

Another step.

We're almost toe to toe now, and I can feel the heat from his body, smell the clean, subtle scent of his cologne—leather and something darker, like storm-wet stone. My chin lifts a fraction higher.

"What's the matter, Dante?" I whisper. "Worried I might know what I'm doing?"

Something flickers in his eyes. A warning. A spark.

And then—he rocks back.

Just a fraction of a pace. Barely noticeable. But I see it.

I *feel* it.

Power, hot and electric, floods me. Not the kind you steal through backdoors and data leaks. Not the kind you broadcast through encrypted channels. This is personal. *Immediate*. This is me, forcing the predator to blink first.

But the moment is razor-thin.

Because he regroups just as fast.

In a blink, he's in front of me again, hand at my throat—not choking, just holding. Reminding. The collar around my neck hums as if reacting to his touch.

His breath is hot against my cheek, and the way he looks at me now isn't the same. It's not cold calculation. It's need. Frustration. And something else that looks a lot like—

"You have no idea what you're playing with," he says,

voice low and raw. "And I don't remember giving you permission to use my name."

"Maybe I do have some idea what I'm playing with," I say, breathless. "And also we're not in a scene. Is that what it's called?"

His thumb drags lightly along my jaw, slow, possessive. "That's where you're wrong. We're *always* in a scene. You want to top from the bottom now, little thief? See if you can tame the monster?"

"No," I murmur, leaning just enough into his hold to make my point. "I want to prove that the monster can bleed too."

There's a beat of silence. One breath. Two.

Then he lets go.

Steps back.

Again.

And this time, *he stays there*.

"Training's done for today," he says, voice rougher than usual. "Go. Cool off."

I should feel dismissed. Controlled.

But I don't. I feel victorious.

And when I walk past him, I keep my chin high, my spine straight, and the memory of his hesitation burns like a brand between my shoulder blades.

Dante O'Driscoll is cracking.

And I'm the queen wielding the hammer that's driving in the wedge.

CHAPTER 10

Dahlia

The terrace is quiet, the night air thick with warmth, toxic smog rising from street level and the scent of rain that never came.

I pick at my food—something obscenely expensive, hand-delivered by one of Dante's faceless minions. Truffle-dusted steak, saffron potatoes, and some kind of air-whipped mousse I couldn't pronounce if I tried.

Personally, I prefer black-market ramen with hot-sauce packets and a stolen view of the skyline. But I don't say that. Not tonight.

I feel a crescendo coming.

Because he's watching me.

Dante O'Driscoll—barefoot, shirt unbuttoned halfway down his chest, charcoal-gray eyes unreadable—leans against the stone railing like a god surveying his kingdom. Hair rumpled. Sleeves rolled. Whiskey untouched.

He's not eating much either and for the first time, he's a little disheveled.

It could be curious if it wasn't so fucking unfair that he looks even hotter than normal.

I swirl my wine, disgruntled. Restless. So fucking horny. Deciding if I'll turn full brat if he decides to send me to bed without the fucking he's been promising for days now.

"So. You gonna tell me why you really need me for this heist, or are we still pretending I'm just here for your entertainment?"

A slow smile. But there's something behind it this time—tension pulling at the corners of his mouth.

"I told you. You're good," he says, then adds, "And it amuses me to have you close. It's only been a handful of days. You have way more begging to do."

I roll my eyes, holding the warm compliment at bay. "You've got a hundred hackers on payroll who can do what I do. Hell, half of them trained at the same black-ops ghost school you probably fund under three shell companies."

He doesn't respond. For a minute, the only sound is the low hum of the city below, the occasional long blare of a horn.

Then he says, almost too softly, "I told you. They're not you. And they didn't steal from me."

Something shifts. His posture stays relaxed, but the edges fray. His fingers twitch against the glass, like he's remembering something he doesn't want to.

I set my fork down. "What happened to you?" It's bald and bold but fuck it.

That flicker. His jaw tightens. A vein pulses near his temple. "Don't," he warns.

"Don't what?" I press, my voice barely a whisper. "Ask why a man who bathes in blood and money and happily exploits the weak suddenly wants justice over his comrade assholes? Because that's what this is, isn't it?" I probe.

The way he seems rabid about this thing succeeding has plagued me for days. Dante isn't doing this just to get one over an enemy. This feels... personal. *Intensely.*

His jaw tightens. For a second, I think he's going to snap at me—say something cruel, something cold, something to remind me exactly who the fuck he is. But he doesn't.

He just stares.

The city lights flicker in his eyes, and I realize he's not looking at me anymore.

He's somewhere else.

"My reasons don't concern you," he says finally, but the edge in his voice is dulled, like he's tired of lying—maybe even to himself.

I tilt my head, watching him. "Everything about me is on your screen. My name. My history. My limits. You even know what toys I've clicked on in that app. You've seen every mask I wear. But you... I thought I knew everything about you." I take a breath. "But here you are, presenting me with a shiny black box of secrets."

Dante shifts, gaze flicking to the skyline, then back to me. "And you should leave it alone. There are things you don't want to know, Specter."

He uses the name like armor. Like a shield.

I smile. But it's not real. And that warmth? It's receding. "You mean things *you* don't want me to know."

He doesn't deny it. And that's when I see it. Another flicker. A deeper shadow. A crack in the diamond-cut mask he wears like skin.

It passes through him like a storm cloud—quick, but enough to darken everything. His eyes go flat. Not emotionless. Worse. *Haunted.*

His mouth opens. "She—" he begins. Then stops. Swallows it.

"Who?" I ask, softer now, almost scared to breathe in case it disturbs the trickle-flow of his giving.

His fingers drum once on the edge of the table, restless. "Someone who thought she could make the world better."

He looks at me—really looks—and for a second, I see it flash behind his eyes: *Pain. Loss. Rage.* A name, maybe. A memory. Something carved deep and ugly into him. "She died for it." There's a pause long enough to bleed. "You of all people should know how that feels."

The reference to my mother is meant to distract, possibly wound. A digital vigilante who died for her cause.

I hate that it achieves both.

He stands abruptly and downs the whiskey in one practiced tilt. "And that's all you get." He straightens, voice smooth as ever. "Finish your wine, Specter. I'm not done with you yet."

He turns to go.

But before he reaches the terrace door, I say, "If you want my cooperation, don't treat me like I'm your enemy, Dante." *Even though you're mine.*

He stops, his shoulders tense. Then, over his shoulder, he says in a voice stripped raw, "Everyone's my enemy eventually."

And he leaves me there—still, burning, and full of questions.

Yes, the moment has vanished. But it was there. I saw it.

Whatever Dante's hiding... it matters.

And I plan to find out.

* * *

BAD GIRL DILEMMA

THE PLAYROOM WAITS for me like it always does—dim and humming with anticipation. Walls of cool steel and shadow. Black leather restraints coiled like snakes. The faintest scent of cedar and sweat and unfulfilled sex lingers in the air.

I step inside barefoot half an hour after dinner, feeling every brush of the cool floor against my warm soles. My dress slips off easily. I left my shame somewhere between the second night and the third orgasm I never got to finish.

But this feels different.

He's already there, dressed in all black, leaning against the padded bench like he owns gravity.

Dante's hot black eyes drag down my body slowly—my small, curvy frame, the flare of my hips, the swell of my breasts. He pauses on my thighs, then moves lower. "You followed the plug instructions." The ones he texted me before dinner.

I nod. The larger stretch is still new, tight and pulsing.

Dante pushes off the bench and circles me like I'm prey. "And the rest?"

I lower my eyes. "Yes, Sir."

Of all the minute things he's let slip, his immediate, electric reaction to that title is the most evident.

It tastes like surrender. *Mine*. Like sin. *Ours*. Like something I don't want to need—but I do.

With the barest flare of his nostrils, he comes closer, tilts my chin up with one finger. "More words, Specter."

I swallow. Wish he would call me Dahlia but I don't vocalize that. "I strip on command. I ask before touching myself. I follow the rules."

His eyes narrow. "Except when you don't."

I tense.

"I know you just tried to hack the tablet again ten minutes ago."

My stomach flips. The collar around my neck seems to pulse with heat. "I just wanted to see—"

He shuts me up with a kiss.

Not gentle. Not violent. Just... *total*.

His mouth takes mine like it has every right to. Like it's been waiting for this moment. Tongue sliding deep, slow, possessive. His hands grip my waist, fingers sinking into my skin like he's memorizing my curves, inch by inch.

I moan before I can stop it.

And he grins against my lips. "Still think you're not fucking mine? That you can do what you please?"

I don't answer. I can't.

Because he's behind me in the next breath, hands firm on my hips, his voice a whisper at my ear. "On the bench. Knees apart. Show me where it hurts."

I obey.

The leather's cool under my skin. I spread my legs, face flushed, my heart hammering as he kneels behind me. His fingers trail down my spine, then dip between my thighs. He strokes lightly, nowhere near enough. One stroke, glancing my clit, my hole.

"You're wet," he murmurs. "Already? From just a kiss? Or from something else? Something that feels like rebellion but tastes like your impending surrender?"

I shudder. Hate how true it is.

But then his hand stills. "Answer me, Dahlia," he says quietly, "Or you don't get fucked."

"No," I whisper, not even sure whether I'm begging him not to deny me or I'm denying him a proper response. Five days of edging have me out of my fucking mind.

He waits.

I squeeze my eyes shut. "From everything," I eventually sigh. "You've kept me waiting for so long. I don't... I can't..."

His large, warm hand glides down my back. Almost

soothing but not quite. "I'm going to fuck you tonight. You've earned it."

Oh God. Please. "Yes, Sir."

He unzips his pants, and I hear the soft jingle of metal.

Then I feel it. Something heavy. Pressing. Hot.

I glance back—and see it.

Holy shit.

His cock is long, heavy, thick, veined and *pierced*. Curved toward his navel. A barbell glints at the head, gleaming with anticipation. Five more decorate his jaw-dropping length. One on top of his corona.

My breath catches. "You didn't tell me—"

"You didn't ask."

"I… I've never—"

"Shhh. Let me teach you."

He crouches in front of me, cups my jaw and kisses me again—slower this time. Gentler. But it only makes the burn inside me worse. Push and pull at full strength.

"You remember your safe word?"

I nod.

He waits. "Say it, so I know."

"Killswitch," I whisper.

He smiles. "Good girl."

He kisses me again, and God, the way Dante uses his tongue and teeth and lips wrecks me. I never thought I'd crave the decadent sounds of our mouths melding like I do now. And for a man who is a master of control and stillness, I love how his hands don't stop moving over my body.

A rumble builds in his chest as his fingers glide down my throat, lingering on the collar for several beats before exploring my collarbones. Testing my strength.

Then my nipples are caught. Pinched. Tugged. Pain upon pain exploding into pleasure. My wince and cry make his eyes gleam. Those eyes that never close chasing my every reaction.

I'm panting. A needy mess by the time he rises and repositions himself behind me. Taps the base of the plug. Electricity zaps through me.

"I'm taking this out now. I'm too big to leave it in for our first time."

I clench my jaw against telling him to leave it. To give me the pain with the pleasure. But even I know that's foolish. Risky. Recklessness might get me fuck all. Or fucked not. I signed a paper that said I would obey.

Surrender.

So I nod. "Yes, Sir."

Did he just tremble? I—

He taps the base again.

"God, please…"

"Tell me how you feel, Little Dahlia," he croons.

We're in double digits now with the *little* now. I'm getting an idea of how I can pay him back. I just need to bide my time. "Electric. Fireworks. Everywhere."

"Surely you can do better than that, Specter?"

"God, just… just fuck me."

Tap tap tap tap tap tap.

One finger hooks through my collar as he taps out a rhythm. A reminder of who's in charge. Who controls my pleasure. Action and consequence. Obedience and reward.

I grit my teeth and pleasure and discomfort detonate through my bloodstream.

"Beg for it."

I remember what he said to me the first night. The threat and promise. "Please!"

"More."

"Please. Please, Sir. Fuck me."

Another long minute. *Tap tap tap.* Then I feel him grip the base.

"Breathe out, baby. Long and slow."

I let out every ounce of air trapped in my lungs. Shudder when he pulls the plug out.

Then Dante's hand closes over the collar. Over my neck. Fingers splayed against my carotid.

The kiss of his crown against my pussy makes me both tense and eager. The touch of the barbell against my wetness makes my mouth water.

His fingers tighten, holding me in place.

I catch the faintest indrawn breath.

And then he's inside me—inch by inch, that hard, metal-studded cock stretching me open. It's too much. It's not enough. I whimper as he sinks deep, and the sensation—the pressure, the fullness, the faint tug of the piercing—makes my eyes roll back.

He groans. "Fuck, you feel like heaven. Small, fragile. Like you're breakable. But you're not, are you?" he grates.

I grip the bench. Roll around in the guttural sound of his second groan. Whimper when his fingers dig into my neck and my hips. He's too fucking big. It fucking hurts. And I love every inch of him I can take and the many I can't.

What I don't love? He's stilled.

I feel his cock beating like a heartbeat inside me. I can't turn my head or move my body. I'm fully under Dante O'Driscoll's control. Can barely breathe. And it's heaven and hell.

"God—please—Sir!"

But he doesn't move.

He just stays there, buried deep, one hand at my throat, the other slipping between my thighs, pressing just above my clit until I'm writhing.

"Come when I say," he growls. "Not before."

My body betrays me. Muscles tighten, everything coils.

But I hold on.

For him.

For me.

For my reward.

Then he finally pulls back. Thrusts. It's deep and devastating. Each stroke hits something primal, and the piercing sends jolts of electric pleasure right through me.

I scream. I beg beg beg. I break.

Dante brings me repeatedly to my peak. Withdraws. Edging me until I'm a sobbing, clawing mess.

"I knew you were worth the wait. Fuck." He says that almost to himself. A smug observation as he pistons in and out. In and out. Beating my pussy like his own percussion drum. A symphony he composes to his exacting standards.

My words dry up and I fall into a trance. Circling the rim of pleasure so acute the line dissolves. I don't know whether I'm dying or resurrecting.

"Sir... please. Let me come," I wheeze. Because his hands relax around my throat.

Dante is owning me. Deciding when I can breathe.

Every thrust amplifies how shamefully wet I am and how I could come just from the decadent sounds alone.

"You hear that, little thief? That's the sound of your cunt begging for me. Acknowledging its Master." His voice is dark velvet, soaked in heat and dominance, like sin spoken into skin. "That's the sound of a good girl being broken in exactly the way she needs."

He tightens his grip—just a little. Enough to make the air catch in my lungs, enough to spike the dizzy euphoria spiraling through me. My body clenches around him like he's the only anchor I have left in a world gone molten and mad.

"You think I didn't see it?" he growls against my ear.

"How wet you were just from my voice? From my command?"

I moan—no, sob—as the truth slams into me harder than any thrust could. He's right. I *craved* this. I *hate* that he knows.

Dante's cock drills deeper, dragging a fresh wave of slick heat from me as he rocks into my soaked, needy core. "Look at you, Dahlia," he pants, fucking me into delirium. "Slick. Shaking. Wrecked. And still hungry for more."

Each word pushes me closer to the edge. He's not just inside my body—he's inside my mind. And I've never felt more *owned*.

I spasm around him. He hisses. Grips my neck and pushes me down until my shoulders and breasts are plastered on the bench.

The angle intensifies… everything.

He's deeper. Fatter. And… and… fuck, I feel the metal stroke a spot that showers my vision with fireworks. "God! Right there! Please, Sir. Right there!"

His breathing escalates. His grip, bruising. "You attempting to steal something else, little thief? To drain my balls for this tight, greedy little pussy before I'm ready?"

Yes. God, yes! "O-only if you want to g-give it to m-me, Sir," I manage.

His rhythm catches fire. Supersonic. He shuttles words and thoughts clean out of my mind.

Then, just when I know I'm going to break his rule, Dante swells inside me, fingers digging cruel and deep into my hips.

"Fuck! Come for me," he growls. "Now."

And I do.

With a scream that tears through the room, through my ribs, through whatever armor I have left. It crashes like a fucking tsunami—violent, wet, and messy.

It's not just an orgasm—it's a detonation.

My whole world blinks white. My muscles seize. My heart stops. Then slams back into motion, faster, freer.

When the spasms fade and I collapse bonelessly beneath him, he stays there—buried deep, still pulsing, still hard.

Then he follows with a roar, pulling me tight to him as he spills inside, shaking with restraint and release.

We collapse together on the bench, breathless. Sticky. Shattered.

"Mine, little thief. Mine," he insists, kissing the corner of my mouth with terrifying gentleness.

And I don't say no.

Afterward, he doesn't speak.

But he doesn't leave either.

And if I wasn't so unhinged with pleasure, *that* would've terrified me.

CHAPTER 11

Dante

She's asleep.

Sprawled across the rumpled black sheets of the playroom bed, her limbs lax, lips parted. Her hair's a dark halo against the pillow, and her skin glows in the low light—marked by my hands, my mouth. The collar gleams at her throat like a brand.

She's still flushed from what we did.

From what I *let* myself do.

I should leave. I always leave.

But I don't.

So many firsts with her. Like fucking without a condom. I was stunned when she ticked the box about no protection. Stunned and relieved, because I sense I would've slipped up and fucked her raw anyway. The joy of reverse hacking my little thief is that I know everything about Dahlia. More than is wise, probably.

I know the last time she was fucked—two years ago. Know the exact location of the shithead too. He's not a threat so I'm leaving him alone. For now.

I stand there like a fucking idiot, pants still half-undone, sweat cooling on my back, staring at the girl I swore I'd break—and wondering if maybe she's the one breaking me.

I turn, move to the console. Pretend I'm checking something. Anything. But my eyes keep drifting back to her. Her body. Her goddamn *face*. I still feel the exquisite clutch of her pussy around my cock. Each stroke a lock finding a key. Each second inside her a homecoming.

Fuck.

I crave a repeat more than my every lifelong wish. Combined.

It wasn't supposed to go like this. Not tonight. Not ever.

She moaned my name like it meant something. Her cunt clenched around my cock like it didn't want to let go. She came so hard I thought I'd have to hold her down to stop her from floating away.

And I felt it. That thing I swore I'd buried years ago.

Need.

Not just the kind that rips through you and demands you drain your balls. I've mastered that kind of want. I've controlled it, weaponized it. Used it to rule boardrooms and boiler rooms to blackmail assholes.

But this…

This is something else.

Something slower. More dangerous. A slow-moving avalanche.

Beautiful, mesmerizing but deadly.

I move to the liquor cabinet across the room and pour myself two fingers of Oban. The single malt burns down my throat, sharp and clean. I watch her the whole time, her back rising and falling in a soft rhythm. Her hand twitches in her sleep like she's reaching for something. Someone.

For me?

No. Fuck no.

I take another sip and set the glass down harder than I mean to.

Because I can't stop thinking about the other thing that has me riled. The revelation out on the terrace. The other *someone*. My sister.

Rina.

About the last time I let someone inside.

It's been six years.

Six long, brutal years since she died. Since the Vesper Syndicate carved a warning into her body and left it on my doorstep like a gift wrapped in horror. She was nineteen. Bright. Reckless. Full of fire and code and stupid, stupid hope.

She'd gotten too close to something she didn't understand.

Just like *her*.

Just like Dahlia.

Except Dahlia understands everything. She's smart in ways that scare me. Clever in ways I didn't prepare for. She walks into rooms she knows are traps and still dares you to spring them.

And when she kneels... when she obeys... when she opens her thighs with trembling pride—

It fucking *undoes* me.

Even suspecting she's faking half of it. I know she's playing a long game. She's a thief, a manipulator. She's lied to every face she's ever shown the world, and I'd be an idiot to think I'm any different.

But the other half?

The part that looks at me like I'm more than a monster?

Like she could consider trusting me with her goals and her needs and her surrender?

I want to believe it. God help me, I do believe it.

I sit on the bench across from the bed and just... *watch*. One arm slung over the backrest. Drink in hand. My chest still heaving like I just came inside her all over again.

I should hate her.

She breached Obsidian's firewalls. She touched *that* folder. She got too close to Ironveil—*again*. I should be punishing her, not laying her down like she's mine. Watching her like she's a fucking oracle.

But she *is* mine. For the next twenty-something days.

That thought hits me like a bullet. No blood, just impact.

She's mine in a way that makes my skin feel too tight.

Mine in a way I never allowed anyone to be after Rina.

Because Rina believed in people.

I stopped. Went dark. Obsidian black.

I've spent the last six years destroying the men who took her from me. One by one. Patiently. Brutally. I dismantled the Vesper Syndicate until their name was a whisper in the dark. But ghosts still haunt and harm.

And now?

Now I'm teaching the one piece of collateral they never accounted for how to wear a plug and beg for my cock like it's her salvation.

Because that's what Dahlia is.

Collateral damage.

She doesn't know it yet, but the heist I'm planning—the one I've coerced her into executing—is the final strike in a war she was never meant to be part of. A war she's bleeding in now, just for being in the wrong place. With me.

But what happens when the game ends?

When I've burned the last of the Vesper Syndicate's legacy to ash and I can finally fucking breathe?

What happens to her?

I drag a hand down my face and let my head fall back against the chair.

She should be a tool. A bystander. A forgotten footnote.

But I want to tell her.

Everything.

She asked why tonight and I came within a whisker of cracking open my most sacred secret. I want to peel open the scar of Rina's name and show Dahlia the rot underneath. I want to whisper every secret into her ear while she's naked and trembling and tied to my bed.

And that's how I know I'm fucking losing it.

Because wanting to expose my secrets?

That's not strength. Not control.

That's fucking surrender.

And the man I used to be—before Rina, before Ironveil, before the blood-soaked empire—died a long time ago.

I'm not that man anymore.

I can't be.

Because Dahlia is a thief. A manipulator. A *target*. And I'm the one holding the detonator.

I get up and cross the room. Stand over her. Just watch. Waiting for this insane feeling to pass so I can feel inhuman, *myself* again.

Her lashes flutter. Her lips part. She murmurs my name like it's a lullaby.

Fuck. My fingers twitch. Damn need. But I don't touch her.

But wanting to, so much, this much? Fuck no.

I back away like she burned me. Because she *will*.

If I'm not careful, she'll ruin everything I've built.

* * *

Dahlia

THE WATER IS HOT, sharp needles against my skin.

I close my eyes, letting it run over the aches Dante put in my body last night.

My thighs are still tender. My lips, still swollen. My insides, still quivering like they remember the stretch of him. The way his cock beat inside me like it wanted to take control, not just of my pleasure but my very heartbeat.

Because how could I forget any of it?

He kissed me like he owned my mouth. Took me like he had something to prove. And afterwards—after I'd cried out for him and given him every broken sound I had—he stayed.

He stayed.

No one ever stays. Not friend or foe. Not even Dad. When it came right down to it, he chose the weighty blankets of grief and pain and memories over his child.

I'm still trying to decide what that means when the shower door opens and Dante steps in, naked and predatory and utterly unapologetic. His charcoal-gray eyes drag down my body like he's already deciding which part to mark again first.

Water beads on his skin, rolls down the taut planes of his abs, glistens around the thick, pierced cock already rising between us.

"Morning," I say, voice sticky with sleep and sarcasm.

"On your knees, Specter."

A flash of heat shoots between my legs but I narrow my eyes. "No coffee first?"

"You'll earn it."

Of course I will.

But I'm already kneeling, eager excitement the steam curling around me as he steps closer. My heart jackhammers. I should be used to this by now—his bluntness, the way he doesn't ask. But there's something about doing it here, under the bright heat of morning, that makes it feel realer.

Rawer.

More mine.

His fingers sink into my damp hair. Tighten. Reminding me of his ownership.

His other hand holds his engorged dick an inch from my salivating mouth. And we both still. Until he nods. Gifting permission.

I wrap my eager hand around the base of him, guiding him toward my lips. I lick slowly, from root to tip, tasting the clean salt of his skin.

The cool metallic tang of his barbells against my teeth. Weird. Wonderful. Absurd and addictive.

I lap lap lap. Moaning for more.

His breath hitches, the only crack in his titanium armor. "Eyes up," he growls. "I want to watch you worship."

I meet his gaze. His pupils are blown wide. Hungry. Possessive.

I take him deeper and feel the weight of him on my tongue. My lips stretch around his girth, and I swear I hear him hiss through his teeth.

"Fuck... that mouth," he rasps. "You're *addicting*, Dahlia."

The word slams into me harder than his cock ever could.

Addicting.

My gut flips. Something sharp and terrifying blooms in my chest. Because he didn't mean to say that. His voice was too raw. Too honest.

And it *hurts*—the way my body thrills at it, sharp and deadly, like cutting yourself on the deadliest blade. The way it makes me feel seen and wanted and so stupidly fragile I almost choke.

So I cover it up the only way I know how.

I pull back and smirk, licking his tip like a lollipop. "You say that to all your criminal conquests, Daddy?"

He barks a laugh. "No," he says, voice hoarse. "You're the first thief who sucks cock like it's revenge."

I swirl my tongue around the head in answer, then take him deep enough to make his legs tense.

"Fuck," he mutters. "Keep going. Don't stop."

And I don't.

I find a rhythm, hands working with my mouth, sucking him until his head falls back against the tile and he groans my name like it's a fucking confession.

"Such a good little thief," he grits out. "So fucking eager. You love it when I use your mouth, don't you? Bet your pussy's dripping just from this."

I moan around him, and he loses it.

"That's it, baby. Suck it just like that. Jesus—your mouth's like sin."

His voice roughens, frays. "Shit—Dahlia—" His voice breaks on the next word. "Gonna come. Gonna fucking come down your throat. That what you want? You want Daddy's come choking you?"

His abs clench. His thighs shake.

"Fuck—yes—goddamn it, just like that, fuck—I can't—"

When he finally comes—thick and hot against my tongue—he pulls me up and slams his mouth onto mine. No hesitation. Just possession. As if the taste of himself on my lips only turns him on more.

The kiss is savage. His hands grip my ass, his tongue relentless. I melt into him, even though I know I shouldn't. Even though I swore I wouldn't.

Afterward, he lathers soap in his hands and starts washing me. Efficient. Focused.

But when he kneels to clean between my legs, his fingers slide in slow and deep, like he's reminding me who owns me now.

I squirm. Moan.

He smirks. "Still sore?"

"Yes, Sir," I breathe. Shaky, hips rolling into his seductive strokes.

"Good. I like you wrecked."

I gasp when his tongue joins the cleaning process.

My hands land on Dante's shoulders, my eyes drowning in obsidian black and he strokes and licks my pussy, coaxing another soul-shaking surrender.

"Come for me, little thief," he croons.

And heaven fuck it all. I whimper and shudder and come.

Once I'm clean, he steps out and grabs a towel, drying me off with practiced care. Like I'm not a criminal he's keeping under lock and collar.

Like I'm... something else.

"What are we doing today?" I ask, just to distract myself from weighty emotions.

"It's the weekend," he says simply, sliding the collar into place around my throat. "We're taking the day off."

My breath catches as the clasp clicks shut. The weight of it feels heavier today. Not physically, but emotionally. Like it means more now. Like I don't know where the game ends and something real begins.

He sees the flicker of emotion on my face, but doesn't press.

Just leans in and murmurs against my ear, "You'll keep it on, little thief. All day. You'll eat with me, walk with me, exist with me. And everyone will know exactly who you belong to."

I swallow hard. My pulse flutters. Because there's no pretending anymore. Not when my body obeys him before my mind catches up.

Not when I *want* the collar.

And definitely not when part of me is scared to take it off.

CHAPTER 12

Dahlia

"We're going out."

It's purely psychological, I know, but the collar turns anvil-heavy the second Dante says those three words.

It's not just the snug fit of the gold against my throat, or the subtle heat of the tech embedded inside. It's the weight of what it means in the absence of distractions.

Obedience. Ownership. Submission.

Inside the penthouse, it's been a game—a twisted, scorching, beautiful game where the rules are brutal but clear. But out there? In the real world?

Wearing this thing outside feels like surrendering and exposing something I'm not sure I can ever reclaim.

I sit on the edge of the bed, towel wrapped around me, staring at my reflection in the dark glass window. My skin is still damp from the shower. My lips swollen. My thighs aching from last night. From him.

And inside, everything's chaos.

Because I heard what he said. Or more accurately, what he *didn't* say.

Last night on the terrace, when I pressed him about why a man like him—filthy rich, corrupt, colder than sin—wanted to pull off a heist that smells suspiciously like justice... he cracked.

Just for a second. Enough for me to see it. Pain. Rage. Grief?

Ironveil. Wraith. *She died for it...*

Who died?

Those were puzzle pieces he didn't mean to drop. But they're floating in my brain now, clicking into place whether he likes it or not. And maybe that's why he clings so tightly to control.

Maybe his darkness isn't just dominance. Maybe it's *defense*.

A fortress built around a wound he's never let heal.

Still, when he lays the clothes out for me—black silk mini dress, no bra, leather heels, delicate gold anklet that matches the damn collar—I stiffen.

"You expect me to wear *this* out there?" I ask, standing, fists clenched around the towel.

Dante doesn't even look up from where he's adjusting the cuffs of his shirt. Dark gray, perfectly tailored. Sharp enough to slice through steel.

"We settled this. You'll wear what I choose," he says evenly. "You knew that the moment you signed your limits list."

I remember that damn list. I remember ticking "Public Play" with my heart racing and my hand shaking.

I didn't expect to *want* it. Not like this.

Not after last night. Not after he kissed me like I wasn't a thief. Like I was *his*. Not after this morning when he called me addictive like he was alarmed and exhilarated. Not after he came down my throat like he was delivering benediction.

"I didn't think you'd actually..." I trail off, heat creeping up my neck. "People are going to see."

He finally looks up.

His eyes are unreadable. Cold. Until they soften, just for a heartbeat.

"Indeed. They'll see what I want them to see," he murmurs. "That you belong to me."

The words lance through me. I should hate that. I should scream at him, spit in his face, slam the door and walk out barefoot just to prove I still can.

But I don't.

Because the truth is, my body likes belonging to him. The same body that used to flinch at every demand now aches when he walks away. The same mind that was once so sure of its own independence now finds a strange safety in the structure of his control.

And maybe that terrifies me most of all.

Still, I lift my chin. "I wear this dress, this collar... it doesn't mean I've submitted."

"No," he says, stepping closer. "But it means you're choosing not to fight me. At least not today."

And that is fucking that. Because he's right. Again.

He helps me dress. No words. Just fingers zipping silk, smoothing fabric, adjusting my hair so the collar is clearly visible. Every brush of his touch is a quiet reminder: *I'm watching. I see you.*

When I finally meet my reflection again, I don't see a thief.

I see something darker. Something bolder.

Someone who might be falling.

He offers his hand. "Shall we, little thief?"

I hesitate. Terrified. Because that sounds less of an accusation and more of a caress. A fond endearment.

Then I slip my fingers into his.

* * *

Dante

She walks one step behind me.

Just like I told her to. Just like she agreed to, with a flash of defiance and a husky "Yes, Sir."

The collar is gold against her throat, glittering in the late morning sun like a promise. Or a warning. The silk dress I picked clings to her curves in all the right places, swaying with each hesitant step. She's trying to look casual, to keep her eyes up, shoulders straight.

But I can see it.

The flush on her cheeks. The tension in her neck. The way her thighs brush together like she's hyper-aware of what's *not* beneath the dress.

No bra. No panties.

Just my rules. My cum still lingering in her mouth from the shower. Her cum still lingering inside her from her surrender.

Mine.

We stroll into the glass-and-steel lobby of a private art gallery I own under a shell company. It's closed for the weekend, save for the two security guards I instructed to disappear before we arrived.

I like my toys like I live my life. Private.

But I want her seen. Her fire is too beautiful to hide under the bushel of my sins.

She walks beside me now, eyes scanning the walls, drinking in the paintings, the sculptures, the obscene wealth it all represents.

I built this place as a front, but also a distraction. A curated illusion of taste and control.

Today, she is the only masterpiece I care about.

"I can feel you watching me," she murmurs, not quite meeting my gaze. I smile. Stunned when my face doesn't crack into a thousand pieces. "Good. Because I am."

Her dark blue eyes flick toward me, a challenge beneath the nerves. Her lips are still kiss-swollen. Her scent—clean skin, arousal, something I'm starting to crave like fucking oxygen—lingers in the air between us.

Her arm rises, fingers brushing the collar. "People could've seen," she says, but there's no fire of protest. Hell, there might even be a little wonder in there.

"They still might."

Her breath catches. I hear it. The way she hates how much that idea turns her on.

Good. Let her squirm. Let her know I own more than her time and her body. I'm owning her mind now, too.

We pause in front of a painting. Something abstract, blood-red and smeared with the anguish of a man who's lost everything. I wonder if she sees it.

"Why are you doing this?" she asks softly.

The question curls between us. A fucking landmine. I keep my expression blank. "Define 'this.'"

"You know what I mean. This whole heist. The plan. The war you're starting. And don't tell me to mind my business again. I'm going to keep asking."

I could lie.

I could tell her it's about power. Money. Revenge.

But then I look at her—*really* look—and that soft fucking voice in my head whispers her name, not her codenames, past or present.

Dahlia.

She's not the girl I kidnapped. Well, not entirely. She's something else now. Something I'm not sure I'll be able to give up.

Even if I have to.

I look away first. Because if I don't, I might tell her the truth.

That I've spent five years plotting every way to destroy them and the systems that protect them. Only to hit a wall. That my enemy's last bastion is proving… impenetrable.

That I need *Dahlia* to help me do it.

Because she's the only hacker alive with the skill set I need… and the only person I can't seem to think straight around anymore.

"I'm doing it," I say at last, "because someone has to."

"Then at the very least tell me who I'm dealing with. Test runs lose their value eventually."

Before she can push again, my phone vibrates.

Encrypted signal. Vesper server. I unlock it with my thumbprint. Then I go very still.

Vesper Syndicate has located Subject S-7.

The message is followed by a low-res surveillance photo.

It's fucking Dahlia.

Taken from across the building across the street.

Timestamp: last night.

While we were on the terrace. While I was cracking myself open on the strength of a single question from her. Because I couldn't help myself.

My blood runs cold.

They know what she is. Who she is. Which means they know she's helping me.

Fuck. For one insane second, I want to smash the phone into the nearest painting and lock her back in the penthouse and never let her step into sunlight again.

But I don't.

I exhale slowly, slide the phone back into my jacket. Allow the single tremor to have its day moving through me before I shut that shit down.

She notices. Her body tenses, sharp and instinctive. "Problem?" she asks.

"Nothing you need to worry about," I lie.

Because if she truly knows the Vespers are close, *who they are*, she'll run. Or worse. She'll *fight*. She's her mother's daughter, after all. Flying blind and fearless into battle.

And I'm not ready to let her go.

Not yet.

Not when I still need her.

Not when I'm starting to *want* her.

And especially not when it feels like every day I don't fuck her senseless and break this need wide open is a day I lose another part of my deranged soul.

***

Dahlia

THE GALLERY IS BEAUTIFUL, in that high-end, sharp-cornered way that screams curated wealth. The kind of place Dante fits into too perfectly. The kind of place that makes me feel like the performance version of myself.

He walks beside me, a looming presence. Possessive. Not gentle. Just... there. Reminding me.

We move from painting to painting—rich oils, tortured brushstrokes, abstract chaos for people who pretend they see meaning in madness.

I pretend too. But I'm not thinking about art. I'm thinking about him.

That "nothing you need to worry about" was clearly bullshit.

And he hasn't touched me since. It's stupid because that was less than five minutes ago, but my body seems to be counting the milliseconds. Counting and missing him.

I sneak a glance up at him as we pause in front of a painting called *Ascension*. White oil streaked with red. Too much red.

His eyes are focused, but not on the art. He's somewhere else entirely. "You like it?" I ask softly.

His gaze slides back to mine. "It's messy. But honest."

"Like me?" I tease, because I need to pull him back.

His lips curve faintly, but humor doesn't reach his eyes. "You're not messy. You're dangerous."

"And you like dangerous."

His hand trails down my spine, subtle and slow. "I like control."

I feel my pulse stutter, soar, elated because he's touching me again. "Is that why we're doing this today? Because you think you're losing it?"

That gets me a flicker of something. Not quite amusement. Not quite warning. "I'm never out of control."

Bullshit. I don't believe him. Because this moment—it doesn't feel like before. The edges have changed. I glance at the pocket he slid his phone into. Deliberately.

His eyes turn colder, giving me the answer I need.

I'm not even surprised when he abandons the grand tour or whatever this is. An exhibit?

"Come."

He leads me toward one of the gallery's private side alcoves. Less flashy. No cameras.

I follow. Not because I have to. Because I need to see what this version of this riled Dante wants.

Halfway down the hallway, he presses me up against the cool concrete wall. My dress hikes with no preamble. Thighs gripped and splayed. His cock is already out, thick and hard, no warm-up or dirty talk.

Just a push.

A thrust.

A claim.

The best delicious stretch in the world.

My breath hitches, but the fire burns. "This is what we're doing, is it? Reclaiming your control, Sir?"

Thrust. Still. "Shut the fuck up, little thief."

I gasp—but not because of the force or the insult. Because of the emptiness in his eyes.

"Dant—"

His fingers close around my throat. Eyes a dark vortex.

He fucks me efficiently. Deep and hard and precise. His breathing remains steady, controlled. Too controlled.

It's clinical. Like I'm part of a ritual, not a woman.

I wrap my arms around his shoulders, grip tight, digging nails into muscle—but he doesn't flinch. Doesn't react.

This isn't sex. This is distraction.

For him. And maybe for me, too.

He comes with a low grunt, not even kissing me. I clench around him anyway out of sheer need, but my orgasm detonates all the same, unravels me, even while it chases something that isn't here anymore.

When he pulls out, I feel colder than the wall.

He adjusts himself. Straightens my dress. Kisses my temple like a caretaker, not a Dom.

"We should get back," he murmurs.

I nod.

But the silence stretches between us like something shattered and swept under a rug.

And for the first time, I don't want to go back to the penthouse.

I want to know what the hell he's hiding.

CHAPTER 13

Dahlia

The silence in the car is the kind that hisses.

Dante drives, one hand on the wheel, the other resting carelessly on my thigh like nothing's changed. Like he didn't just use my body as a pressure valve and walk away before the emotional steam had cleared.

He hasn't said a word since the gallery. I haven't either.

But I'm not quiet out of obedience. I'm quiet because I'm calculating.

Because something shifted. And now, so will I.

Back in the penthouse, I head straight for the spare room while Dante disappears into his study. Calls to make. His voice is back to neutral, impassive. Professional.

I wait until I hear the low murmur of his voice through the door—then I move.

His room still smells like cedar and power. I walk past the

bourbon decanter, the monogrammed leather folders. His sleek black laptop glows with soft light on the desk.

Unlocked.

Almost like he wants me to look.

I take the fucking bait.

Folder after folder appears on screen—financials, blackmail dossiers, offshore accounts under names I know and some I don't.

And then I see it.

A file I've seen before. The one labeled "Vesper Syndicate: Access Protocol." But just like the other one labeled *Wraith* stopped me in my tracks last time, the one beneath this one freezes my blood.

My breath stutters. Another coincidence? No. Not here. Not now.

I stare at the folder like it might swallow me whole. I've walked into this trap before. But… fuck it. I pummel the firewalls for a quick minute for the Vesper Syndicate file. Enough to see what I'm working with.

Then I double-click.

Predictably, the screen flashes RED.

Unauthorized Access Detected. Lockout Sequence Initiated.

He knew I'd try. He let me find it. My pulse hammers. Baited me, first with *Wraith* and now with my own name.

Specter.

The one I buried years ago, along with my mother. Along with everything soft in me. Until I resurrected it in her name. In her honor.

I click the file with my name.

Encrypted.

Of course. As if that would stop me.

I'm already halfway through the backdoor when I hear the door open. My heart jumps but my fingers don't stop and

I don't look up. Not right away. Because I know whose blazing, lethal eyes are on me.

"What the fuck do you think you're doing?" Dante's voice is low, sharp as a blade.

I don't flinch.

"I asked you a question."

I keep typing. Calm. Careful. Failing. "I think the better question," I murmur, "is what *you're* doing with a folder named after my codename inside one named Vesper Syndicate."

Silence. No movement. But I feel him there—tension radiating off his body like heat from a live wire.

When I finally lift my head, his face is a warzone—fury etched into every brutal line, his jaw clenched so tight it looks like it might shatter.

"You think you're invincible, little thief?" he snarls, voice low and dangerous. "You hack into my system and think I won't chain your pretty little ass to a wall?"

I look at him. And I mean *look*. And for the first time, I don't see a powerful predator, a monster who eats other monsters for breakfast. I see a control freak standing in the middle of an uncontrollable lightning storm, wondering where the next strike will come from.

"I think if you wanted to send me to jail, you'd have done it already. I think even if I hadn't agreed to this thirty-day circus, you still wouldn't have thrown me to the wolves. You're the only wolf you want touching me."

That throws him. Just a second. A flicker of something uncertain behind the anger.

"You don't get to fucking disobey, make demands," he snaps. "Or change terms."

"I'm not demanding." My tone is soft. Even. Dangerous. "I'm asking. Tell me what this is. Ironveil. Vesper. Tell me what my name is doing here. Tell me why it's buried under five levels of encryption and why the files feel like a graveyard awaiting a reaper's scythe."

He says nothing.

I nod once. "That's what I thought." I move to close the laptop.

"You'll know," he says suddenly. "When the time is right."

I freeze. My fingers still rest against the trackpad. "And I'm just supposed to trust you?" I ask quietly.

Dante exhales, long and slow, like he's holding something back. "Yes."

I want to believe him. God, I want to. But the tightness in his voice—the tremor in his restraint—tells me I've seen something I wasn't meant to.

He steps forward.

I stand, laptop still in hand.

We're close now, toe-to-toe. Eye to eye.

"You keep secrets, Dante. I keep plans."

His mouth curves—not a smile. A threat. "Don't test me, Specter."

"Too late."

The stare between us lasts five seconds too long. I feel it in every inch of me. My skin is hot, my stomach tight. The scent of him—leather, smoke, power—invades my lungs. I hate how much I crave it.

So I step back. Not in surrender. In strategy.

"Goodnight, Mr. O'Driscoll."

He doesn't answer.

Just watches me walk out of his study like a woman who didn't just open Pandora's Box.

* * *

The penthouse is quiet.

Too quiet.

Dante hasn't come to bed tonight. I'm not sure if it's restraint or punishment. Or both.

I put the plug in as per my training. And fuck if I don't get myself wet doing it, remembering how thoroughly he fucked me last night, this morning, even in the gallery when he was one level above an automaton.

But I'm not going to let lust derail me.

He said I'd know when the time was right.

The more I think about it, the more I don't know that I believe him.

I curl up on the black leather sofa with a bowl of cereal and his backup tablet. I crack the first layer of the firewall in less than three minutes. Half my focus is on the screen—the other half is on the hallway, listening for footsteps.

He's not coming.

Not yet.

Which means I still have time.

To get deeper. To find out what Ironveil really means. Why the name Specter lives in his files.

And what it has to do with the girl in the photo I found buried in subfolders.

Is she the 'she' he referred to?

Or is she... *it* worse?

I crunch a spoonful of cornflakes and open a new window.

My pulse is steady. My breathing calm. I squirm and the presence of the plug pulses, sending new, salacious ideas on how to tackle this through my depraved brain. If I'm to be mired in lust and surrender, maybe I can use that to my advantage?

My fingers slow and the idea takes hold. Builds.

Shimmers with purpose and possibility.

* * *

Dante

She thinks I don't know.

That I didn't notice the faint shift in her voice when I walked in earlier. The twitch of her fingers over the trackpad, the barely suppressed rush of adrenaline in her pupils.

She was inside the fucking system again in the middle of the night. Rooting around Vesper and Specter.

She's careful, I'll give her that. Cool as polished glass on the surface. But underneath? The vigilante brat throwing a tantrum. She's lit wire and storm surge—reckless when she thinks the risk is worth the reward.

And tonight, she decided *I* was worth it.

I pour myself a glass of Oban, neat, and sit at the edge of the long mahogany desk. Her fingerprints are still on the lid of the laptop. Her scent—vanilla, ozone, something uniquely hers—lingers in the leather chair.

She's getting too close. Too fucking close. And not just to the files.

To *me*.

I've spent years building walls that not even God could breach. But Dahlia?

She keeps finding the cracks.

And every time she kneels for me... the instinct that screams she was right for me flares with pride. Every time she whimpers my name with her lips red and swollen, eyes glassy from submission... I forget why I built the walls in the first place.

I should've shut this down the first night. Should've reminded myself what she is: a thief, a hacker, a professional manipulator. She's playing the long game, and I know it.

I fucking *respect* it.

But it doesn't matter.

Because I'm playing one too.

Tonight, I'll fuck her into a state of ruin so deep she won't be able to remember her goddamn name, let alone her passwords.

And while she's limp and panting and destroyed beneath me?

I'll buy myself time.

Time to move the files. To reroute the triggers. To bury Ironveil and everything it threatens deeper than she can dig. Until the time is right.

Time to figure out how to protect her—from the Syndicate, from what's coming, from herself while using her. Bending her to my will.

Because despite everything, I don't want her broken.

I want her *mine*.

And she can't be mine if she's dead.

I toss back the rest of the scotch and set the glass down too hard. It cracks against the marble.

And fuck, I feel it resonate deep inside me.

She's finding the cracks.

And I'm feeding her the wedges.

* * *

Dahlia

MY HANDS ARE BOUND behind my back, wrists tight with soft leather cuffs that creak when I move. Dante's hand is firm around my throat—his favorite way to keep me still.

His cock pushes inside a pussy throbbing and sore with relentless fucking.

My safe word is a gauntlet writhing between us as his

cock slams into me from behind, every brutal thrust a declaration, a punishment, a filthy kind of love letter written in grunts and wet slaps and the sharp sting of denied pleasure.

"Say it," he growls, voice low and brutal against the shell of my ear. Sweat drips from him, down my temple to the corner of my mouth.

I catch it with my tongue. Moan at my prize.

"Tell me who owns this pussy."

I sob, hips bucking back into him like I'm possessed. "You do—fuck—Sir, you do—please, don't stop—"

He tightens his grip just slightly. Enough to steal the edge of breath from my lungs. Enough to feel the many pulse points on my body.

The heavy chain attached to the harsh clamps spikes pain into each nipple with every movement.

The two beads deep in my ass that rub sublimely against the membrane separating my holes, making me see stars.

The thighs spread perpendicular to the waist-high bench he placed me on so he could fuck me like I'm his human fleshlight.

"No," he says. "I think I'll stop. You haven't earned it."

"No—no, please—" My voice breaks, high and wrecked.

He pulls out.

I scream.

Not loud. Not dramatic. Just that raw, desperate little cry I've never made for anyone else. The one that comes from the deep hollow of my belly. From the place he's carved out just for him.

"You beg like a fucking angel," he says darkly. "But you're still just a greedy little thief. Always taking. Always reaching."

"I'm not—I'm trying—I'm yours, I swear—"

He groans at that.

And then he slaps my pussy, sharp and wet, two fingers parting my folds to find my soaked clit.

"You call this trying? You're dripping all over my cock and you think I'll reward that?"

My knees wobble. I'm barely upright.

But I love it. God, I love it.

"Please," I sob. "I can't—I'll die if you stop—"

He shoves back into me with a savage thrust, and I swear I black out for a second. My head tips forward, head hanging off the bench as I gasp for air.

His rhythm is merciless. "Come now and I'll edge you again for the rest of the fucking night," he grits.

I choke on a moan.

The orgasm teeters, threatens, then fades when he pulls out again.

"You're... this is, Jesus, please! Don't stop," I cry out, broken and shaking. "Please—Sir—I need it—Tell me what you want. I'll do anything—"

"I know," he says, quieter now. And that's the worst part.

He knows how much I crave this. How much I have to give him.

And the devil takes it all.

But when he finally gives it back—when he grabs my throat and slams into me again, cock thick and hot and filling me so deep I can't breathe—I'm nothing but fire and ruin and pure, feral need.

"Now," he growls. "Fucking come now."

I shatter.

It rips through me, my orgasm crashing down so hard my body gives out. He holds me up. Fucks me through it. His breath catches as he follows—cock pulsing deep inside me as he presses his forehead to the back of my neck.

"Fuck," he whispers. "You'll destroy me, long before I destroy you, won't you, little thief?"

I want to tell him he already has.

Instead, I just lie there trembling, leaking surrender, skin marked, soul claimed and body satisfied in the most dangerous way.

I hope I've taken something from him. I hope every moan I gave him tonight stains him forever.

* * *

I WAKE in the middle of the night.

Dante lies sprawled across the bed like a god sculpted from shadows and sin, chest rising in slow, even breaths. His arm's flung across the sheets where my body had been, as if in sleep he still seeks me. The faintest furrow creases his brow. Even unconscious, he's guarded.

But not for long.

Because today, I have a plan. One that requires sweat, stamina, and sex so damn intense he won't be able to see straight. If I wear him down enough, push his mind and body to the brink, I'll buy myself the time I need.

Time to break into Ironveil. Time to find out what Vesper truly is beyond the whispers and smoke I heard about on the Dark Web, and what Specter... *I*... have to do with it.

Slipping beneath the sheets, I breathe him in—sandalwood and smoke and power. He smells like ruin. Like temptation incarnate. I trail my lips down his stomach, watching for movement. His cock twitches once against his thigh.

I smile. Brat mode locked. "Rise and shine, Sir."

I don't give him a chance to protest.

My lips close around the head of his cock, tongue swirling lazily over his barbells as I hollow my cheeks and suck deep.

He grunts awake, eyes snapping open. One hand tangles in my hair, and for a moment, I think he's going to take over. Or stop me. Demand I ask for permission.

But he doesn't.

He watches instead. Silent. Letting me set the pace. Letting me pretend I'm in control.

And gradually, his breath is ragged, hands clenched at his sides like if he moves, he'll lose whatever grip he has left. "You trying to kill me, my filthy little brat?" His voice is morning-rough and ruined, like gravel laced with sin.

I pull back, letting his cock fall from my lips with a wicked pop. I lick my lower lip slow, deliberate. "Not kill. Just weaken. Tear down a few firewalls. Maybe."

His jaw ticks. "Then you'd better finish what you started, and finish good, or I'll flip you over and fuck that smart mouth until you forget your own name."

I hum innocently and stroke him with both hands. "Promises, promises, Sir."

His growl vibrates through the air. His fingers tighten in my hair. Cruel with intent. "Hands off, knees spread, mouth open," he snaps, voice all Dom steel. "You want to play, let's see how well you take cock down your pretty little throat."

I obey, heart pounding, arousal pooling between my thighs.

My quick compliance makes his belly clench, his eyes flare.

Fist clamped in my hair, he drags me onto his cock. Pushes deep and relentless until I'm fully gagged. Eyes watering and breath gone.

He stays, stays, stays, a growl working up his throat. He releases me with a rough exhale. "Is that what you're begging for, little brat?"

"Yes, Sir."

"Then take it. Again. Hands behind your back. Better yet, hands on that luscious ass. Part yourself. Feel how empty you are as you take me down your throat. Now. Let's see how cocky you are without them."

He surges deep. Deeper.

Again. And again.

Until I'm bruised and breathless. A mess of tears and emptiness.

Only then does my Dom release me. Tucks his arms behind his head. "You wanna ride, pet?"

My head is bobbing before I wipe away the drool from his taste. "Please, Sir."

"Bring that cunt over here then," he commands, threading his fingers into my hair. "Fucking ride. And don't stop until I say."

The power—fleeting and ephemeral—may look like mine, but we both know who's really in control. His eyes darken, but before he can change his mind, I climb on top and straddle him. No teasing this time—I slide down slow, taking him inch by inch, until I'm seated flush against his hips.

His mouth parts on a breath. "Fuck."

I ride him hard. Slow. Deep.

My fingers splay across his chest, nails dragging down the perfect lines of muscle. The bed creaks beneath us.

Every step of his Jacob's Ladder is like climbing into heaven. His cock hits places inside me that make me see stars, but I bite down on my pleasure. Not yet.

I lean over him, lips brushing his. "Can I come whenever I want, Daddy? I promise it'll be worth it."

His dick jerks inside me and I want to crow with triumph. I don't. The tables turn far too easily around here.

He laughs, and it's husky and low and addictive. And I allow triumph's dance. "Is that a promise or a threat? For you or for me?"

"Both. All of the a-above!" I yelp when his crown brushes a sublime place, deep inside.

"Come here." Gruff. Commanding. The kind of tone that strips me bare without even touching me.

I lean in closer, brace my hands against the headboard.

The angle makes his cock even more brutal and delicious. My nipples graze his chest, sparking wildfires filled with electricity.

His cock pistons inside me, his upper half barely moving as his stare commands mine.

God, he's so fucking good at this.

With clinical fascination he tracks my gasps and jerks. My moans and shivers.

When my thighs shake from the effort of wringing every ounce of energy from his body he grips my hips, guiding my pace even as I tremble, even as my moans start to sound more like sobs.

"Look at me." His voice cuts through the haze. Sharp. Absolute.

I try. I try to lift my gaze to his, but everything's too much —his cock buried deep, the ache between my legs, the burn and promise of every orgasm he's dragged from me like a confession.

"I said, look at me."

His fingers tighten just enough to make me gasp. "You want your prize, little thief? Then fucking earn it. Come on my cock while holding my eyes. Don't you dare look away."

My breath catches. Panic flickers through me.

I'm not sure I can.

Not because I don't want to—but because everything in me is unraveling. My little game is backfiring. "I can't—"

"Yes, you can," he growls, thrusting up hard. "You're mine. You take what I give you, and you look me in the eye when I ruin and reward you."

And just like that, I shatter.

With his name on my lips, tears slipping down my cheeks, and his slate-grey eyes burning straight through me.

We fuck until we're both dripping sweat, until the sheets

are damp and my thighs shake from the effort of wringing every ounce of energy from his body.

And still, I don't stop.

Because I can't. Because he won't let me. Because somewhere between the thrusts and the commands, I stopped being in control.

And now I'm caught in my own game of destruction—bleeding for a man I was supposed to break.

CHAPTER 14

Dante

She thinks I'm asleep.
That's cute.

I hear the faint rustle of a T-shirt over bare skin. The quiet click of the bedroom door. Her light footsteps down the hall. I rise and follow, naked and feet bare.

In time to hear the telltale clink of a spoon against a bowl. A smile curves my lips before I can stop myself.

Cereal. Always with the fucking cereal.

For a hacker who can dismantle the world's digital skeleton, she still eats like a college dropout. There's something disarmingly honest about it. Something that makes it hard—impossible—to keep my distance.

I stay still in the hallway for another minute, just breathing. Already missing her. The sheets were warm where her body was. My cock aches from the relentless rhythm of her riding me half the night. And even now, my pulse won't settle.

Because she's inside me in ways I didn't fucking plan for.

And I know.

I know she's trying to fucking play me.

She believes if she keeps me satisfied—fucked senseless and sated with her surrender—I won't notice her sneaking around, won't realize how dangerously close she's gotten to the truth.

But I'm doing the exact same thing.

Keeping her under me. Inside me. Around me. As long as I can.

Because the moment she finds out the full truth about Ironveil, about the Vesper Syndicate, about what happened to my sister... everything changes.

The collar. The playroom. The discipline. It's not just about control anymore—it's about protection. My *protection*. Hers.

I told myself I brought her here to keep an eye on her.

To fuck her, use her skills, then cut her loose. But I was lying.

Even then.

Because the second I saw her file in that syndicate database—**Specter S**-7—I knew she wasn't just another target.

She was the ultimate bait. Just as her mother had been.

And if I don't get ahead of this, they'll use her to get to me. Or worse: erase her the way they erased Rina.

Goddamn it.

My body's heavy from too much sex and too little sleep, but I move silently through the penthouse, tracking her to my study.

She's sitting at my desk, her laptop open. Mine's beside it, active. The screen glows blue in the dark. I watch her for a long moment from the doorway, alarmed and deeply thrilled by the sight of her in my seat. Barefoot. Hair a gorgeous mess from our fucking. Knees pulled up into the chair.

Her dark blue eyes are locked onto the scrolling code, her brows drawn in fierce concentration. And fuck me if it isn't the hottest thing I've ever seen.

Adorably obvious as she's hacking me. And I almost let her.

I clear my throat.

She doesn't jump. Doesn't even blink. Just tilts her head and says, "How long have you been standing there?"

"Long enough to ask what the fuck you think you're doing." There's no heat.

She taps another key. Keeps working. "Looking for answers."

"That's my machine, Specter."

"I know," she says, calm. Too calm. "But I need to know what you're hiding."

I laugh, but it's hollow. "What do you think I'm hiding?"

She glances up. "Something about why you play executioner with a god complex."

I clench my jaw. "Careful," I warn. "You're not just breaking the rules—you're pissing on the last line of trust I gave you."

"Then explain it," she says. "Tell me the truth."

"Same answer as before. I'll tell you when it's time."

She leans back, arms folded. Her gaze is sharp, calculating. "That's not an answer."

"No," I agree. "It's a promise."

We stare at each other. Silence, thick and heavy.

I expect her to rage. Threaten. Maybe beg since she's become so damn perfect at it.

But all she does is nod, as if she's just confirmed something.

She's made a decision.

Fuck.

* * *

Dahlia

I LIE ON MY STOMACH, cheek pressed to Dante's chest, the air still thick with the ache of our last scene. My thighs burn in that delicious way only he can orchestrate. Every muscle is loose and my pulse a lazy thrum. His fingers move through my hair, patient and repetitive, as if we have all the time in the world.

We don't.

The days are bleeding together too fast. My internal clock —so reliable in the outside world, when I was nothing but shadow and vengeance—is spinning. And somehow, it's already day fifteen.

Halfway mark.

I should be panicking. Planning my next hack. Scouting my escape. But I just let him touch me.

"You're quiet," he murmurs.

I glance up. His eyes study me the way they always do after a scene. Like he's trying to memorize the wreckage he's caused.

"Just tired," I lie.

He doesn't press. He kisses my forehead instead. Soft. Intimate.

And dangerous.

Because it feels real. Too real.

I feign sleep, wait until his breathing evens out, until his hand falls from my hair and his body slackens. Then I carefully, quietly, slip from the bed. My legs wobble, but I brace against the wall and breathe through it.

I don't look back at him.

If I do, I might not leave the room.

I return to the study. And I begin.

Again.

Two Days Later

I'M in his study again, barefoot and wearing one of his shirts, when he storms in like a thunderclap—suit jacket half-off, tie loose around his neck, and fury burning behind his eyes.

I told myself all through my little escapade that I could withstand the fallout. But now he's striding toward me, fury and intent and... a little panic? I can't quite catch my breath. Can't contain the torrent rushing in to fill the gaping spaces being out of his orbit created.

"You went home," Dante snaps, slamming the door shut behind him. "You slipped through my system, accessed your apartment, and made a call. Who to?"

I blink, fingers still resting on the keyboard. "I didn't realize I needed your permission to go to my own damn home."

"You knew the rules."

"I agreed to thirty days in your bed," I say, rising slowly, my voice calm even as my pulse drums. "I didn't agree to abandon my life. I didn't agree to be erased."

He stalks toward me, jaw tight, energy crackling off him like lightning on metal. "You could've been followed. You compromised the entire op. Do you have any idea what—"

"No," I interrupt. "Because you won't tell me."

He stops. Chest heaving. Eyes narrowed.

"You're… scared. Why?"

A muscle ticks in his jaw. "Stop. Right now."

"No. Why are you so scared?" I whisper. "Why does me going home terrify you?"

"Don't flatter yourself," he growls.

"You track my every move. Collar me. Deny me release, deny me answers. You fuck me like I'm your possession and then panic the second I breathe on my own."

His nostrils flare.

I step closer, place a hand on his chest. "You're not just angry, Dante. You're afraid. I saw it the second you walked in."

He turns his back to me, but I see his shoulders tense. His hand curls into a fist on the desk.

"I went to my apartment," I continue quietly. "I logged in. I checked old messages. Talked to my dad. That's all. Just… trying to remind myself who I was before all this."

Silence.

"I was always going to test the bonds of the chains and the collars. We both know that."

Cold. Heavy. Silence. Eerie and deep.

"I didn't mean to break your trust," I say, and it's not a lie. Not entirely. "But you don't trust me either."

His silence hurts more than his anger. So I change the subject—no, I *weaponize* my pain. My vulnerability. A dagger to his firewalls.

His head shifts, barely, like he's listening. Intently.

"After my mother died," I say, "my father couldn't look me in the eye for six months. She was in the wrong place at the wrong time, because of me. And it tore us apart."

I swallow hard, the memory bitter in my throat.

"He never said it out loud, but I felt it. Every day. Like his silence was a verdict I couldn't escape. I stopped coming home after classes. Started staying out late just so I didn't have to see the disappointment in his face. I think... I think part of him wished I'd died instead of her."

The words hang between us, heavy and raw.

"I tried to be better after that. Smarter. Tougher. But the damage was done. We both wore our grief like armor, but mine cut deeper. Because I knew the truth—if she hadn't been picking me up that night, if I hadn't forgotten my phone —she'd still be alive.

"I know what loss feels like, Dante," I whisper. "That gaping black hole you build your whole life around. And the secrets you'd kill to protect it." I walk to him, place a hand on his back.

"I know you're hiding something. Ironveil. Specter. You pretend to be angry when I overstep but hold me like I'm precious. Even as you look at me like I'm a goddamn ghost."

His shoulders shake. Once.

But he doesn't turn.

"You said you'd been watching me for a long time. That you want my surrender. You want my obedience? You can have all of it, Dante. All I ask in return is that you give me truth."

* * *

Dante

SHE'S TOO SMART.

Too fast.

Too fucking *close*.

When she said her mother died, it gutted me. Because I knew that kind of grief. The kind that rewires your DNA, poisons your sleep, turns you into a monster with a pretty mask.

I still haven't turned to face her.

I can't.

If I do, she'll see it. All of it. I stride to the liquor cabinet without registering it. The glass is in my hand but my fingers are numb.

The pulse of memory, though? It sears, burning everything in its path.

"Ironveil wasn't supposed to exist anymore," I finally say. My voice sounds like it's being dragged through glass. "I buried it after they killed her."

"Her?"

"Rina. My sister."

"Your sister," Dahlia repeats softly. "And they are… the Vesper Syndicate?"

I nod.

"She was nineteen. Bright. Unstoppable. A hacker like you, only cleaner. She thought she could outplay them. And when she tried… they made an example out of her. Filmed it. Made me *watch*. Then they dumped her body on my doorstep."

The room tilts. My knees almost give out.

"She was everything good in me," I say. "And when she died, all I had left was revenge. So I infiltrated Vesper. Learned how they move. Who they bribe. Who they ruin. Ironveil was the failsafe—a lockbox of everything I've collected on them for ten years."

"And Specter?" she asks, voice cautious.

My eyes meet hers. "Specter was… her alias. Before they erased her."

Dahlia steps back like she's been hit.

"I chose you because you carried the name. I thought it was fate. Or maybe just guilt. Maybe I wanted to weaponize you."

I laugh bitterly.

"But you weren't a weapon. You were the *detonator*. Getting too close with every heist. I know you've already heard about them. It was only a matter of time before your little online poll chose them next. I couldn't let that happen."

Her lips tremble. "So that's why you brought me here? That's why I'm in danger?"

"Every other reason still holds. But, yes," I say. "Ironveil is locked, but not impenetrable. And now they know something's moving. You're a liability, Dahlia."

She flinches, and I instantly regret the word.

But then she lifts her chin. "Then let me do what I do. Protect me. Or let me go. But stop withholding."

I step forward. Cupping her face, my thumbs brushing her cheeks.

"I *can't* let you go." The words leave me before I can stop them.

Because it's true. She's already under my skin. Already inside every decision I make.

This started as a game of collateral and revenge.

But now?

Now it's something else entirely.

And we're both standing too close to the fire to walk away unscathed.

* * *

Dahlia

I WAKE to the sound of choking.

Not mine.

His.

Dante thrashes beside me, soaked in sweat, his breaths jagged, panicked. Moonlight cuts across his face and I see the anguish. His lips part like he's trying to speak. A name slips out between clenched teeth. "Rina."

His sister.

My chest seizes.

"Dante," I whisper, brushing damp hair from his forehead. He jerks again, and I press my hands gently to his cheeks. "Wake up. Come back."

His eyes fly open, wild and unmoored.

He grabs my wrists, hard—reflex more than intention. But the second he sees, sees *me*, something in him crumbles.

"I'm here," I murmur. "Just me."

His jaw clenches. "She was screaming," he says hoarsely. "I couldn't stop it. Couldn't fucking move. They made me—made me *watch*."

"I know," I say, even though I don't. Not really.

But I feel it. In every line of his body, the way he's unraveling beneath the surface. Powerless. Trapped. Haunted.

And maybe I'm selfish, or maybe I'm just as broken—but I need him inside me. I need to pull him out of his head and into mine. Need to give him something to control when he's drowning in things he can't.

"Let me help," I whisper, guiding his hand to my throat. "Take what you need. Master me, Sir. Destroy me."

His gaze flickers. Something fierce blooms behind it. His fingers tighten and his cock thickens. Surges.

"On your knees," he rasps.

My pulse kicks.

I slide down the sheets and kneel at the edge of the bed. Naked. Waiting. Wanting.

"Hands behind your back."

I obey. Breathless and grateful.

His cock is hard, jutting from the dark V of his hips, and when I lean forward to take him into my mouth, no preamble. All gloried surrender.

He hisses through his teeth.

"Fuck. That's it," he growls, fingers curling into my hair. Tight enough to sting and bruise. "Take your goddamn penance, little thief."

I hum around his length, hollowing my cheeks, licking along the underside of his engorged cock until his grip tightens.

"Christ. You're so fucking good at this," he mutters. "Like you were *made* to be on your knees for me."

I moan, gag slightly as he pushes deeper.

"Messy. Obedient. Fucking *mine*."

His cock pulses deep in my throat. Once. Twice. But he pulls me off just before he comes, fisting my hair and yanking me to my feet.

"I'm not done with you."

He flips me around, presses my face to the mattress, and shoves into me with a brutal, hungry thrust that knocks the breath from my lungs. "Oh—*fuck*—"

"Say my name," he snarls against my ear, one hand wrapping tight around my throat.

"S-sir."

"No. *Say my name!*"

"D-Dante—" I gasp, voice shattering.

"Louder."

"Dante! Please—oh my *God*—"

"You feel that?" he pants, fucking me harder, deeper. "That's how deep you are in me, Dahlia. In my head. In my goddamn *soul*."

My vision whites out. I sob as he edges me, pulling out at

the last second, denying me the orgasm that's clinging to every nerve.

"Please, please—don't stop—Sir—"

"Milk me with that tight little cunt all you want. You'll still come only when I say."

Tears sting my eyes.

He slaps my ass, grips my hip hard enough to bruise, and drives back into me. "This is the only place I'm sane. Where I find fucking peace. Inside this pussy. Inside *you*. Don't you fucking get it?"

My voice is gone. There's only breath. Heat. Surrender.

Whimper and bracing for the storm.

And when Dante O'Driscoll breaks all over me, I come with a cry, trembling so violently he has to hold me up. His own groan follows seconds later, low and guttural, as he spills and spills and spills inside me.

He collapses over my back. Not crushing—just *there*.

His lips brush my shoulder. "You scare the shit out of me." His voice is low, wrecked—like the truth is a blade he's finally stopped dodging. Or a confession dragged from the ruins of a man who never meant to feel this much.

I swallow. "Why?"

"Because I'd burn the world to keep you safe," he says, breath rough. "And I don't know who I become when that happens."

I twist beneath him. Cup his cheek.

"You're not alone in this, Dante." He dragged me into this —literally kicking and screaming. Now wild horses couldn't drag me out.

And God help me, I don't know if it's because I believe in the mission… Or because I'm too far gone for the man behind the monster.

He looks at me like he wants to say something more. But he doesn't. He just pulls me close. Wraps me up tight in his arms. And for the first time, I feel it—not just sex or surrender or strategy but something real.

Something we don't have words for yet.

Something we both know can't last.

Because the clock is ticking.

And we're running out of time.

CHAPTER 15

Dahlia

I catch myself in the mirror of the penthouse's elevator, my breath catching at the reflection. Me, in sheer black latex, a corset that laces tight up the back, long gloves that reach past my elbows, and the delicate line of the leather collar gleaming around my throat. No underwear. No escape.

The collar feels heavier tonight. Not in weight, but in meaning.

Dante stands behind me, tall and sharp in his obsidian suit, dark eyes locked on mine in the glass.

"Color?" he murmurs, lips brushing the shell of my ear.

I whisper, "Green."

He kisses my temple. "Good girl."

My stomach knots. I don't know if it's dread or desire. Maybe both.

Because tonight, we walk into the belly of the beast. The Gilded Cage—where names don't matter, only power. And we're going hunting.

The head of the Vesper Syndicate, the ghost behind a thousand ruined lives, is here. Dante confirmed it hours ago, combing through private networks of the sex club, triangulating locations. And if we don't make our move now, the trail will go cold.

But what I didn't expect—what I hadn't counted on—is the weight in Dante's voice. The way he watches me like this might be the last time. The desperation under his dominance.

It scares me more than the mission.

* * *

Dante

I shouldn't have brought her.

But the second I thought about leaving her behind, I imagined her going off-script, hacking in without backup, putting herself in danger. Again.

She's under my skin. Under my fucking soul.

And tonight, if things go south, there's no telling how far the Vespers will go to silence her.

Under different circumstances, I would've saved her first real-life visit for when the concrete version of The Club was finished in San Francisco. But even that speaks to a future that widens the cracks inside me.

Focus.

The doors to the members-only club in Lower

Manhattan open to us like a heartbeat—dark, throbbing, seductive.

Red velvet walls, bodies in motion, skin slick and glistening under strobe light. Eyes track Dahlia the moment we step in. Her tits press against the corset like a fucking invitation. But she's mine.

Tonight, everyone will know.

"Stay close," I say, voice low but firm.

"I always do," she murmurs, slipping her hand into mine.

I should feel in control. Instead, I feel like I'm losing it.

* * *

Dahlia

I EXPECTED THE SEX CLUB—SINCE I was a submissive—to make me feel small. To feel overwhelmed by leather and leashes, the pounding bass of want echoing off the walls, the collective hunger in every look.

Instead, it makes me feel *seen*.

Because here, my submission isn't weakness.

It's currency. Power. A declaration of strength in surrender.

Dante's fingers rest lightly on the small of my back as he guides me through the crowd—less a nudge, more a silent tether. Every inch of my body is on display: black mesh corset, no bra, a collar so subtle most wouldn't clock it as what it is unless they knew. And in here, everyone *knows*.

"Eyes up," Dante murmurs in my ear, breath hot. "Confidence, not apology."

I nod and keep moving. Past sin-drenched lounges, curtained alcoves hiding moans and power plays, red-lit rooms where shadows become theater. The scent of sweat and sex clings to the velvet-lined air.

A near-naked server walks us to a curved booth, and Dante helps me into it.

The man loitering near us watches me with too much interest—his eyes skating down my thighs, lingering on the curve of my breast. I feel the heat of Dante's glare before I even look at him.

"Eyes the fuck off," Dante says sharply. The man flinches and vanishes into the crowd.

"Was that necessary?" I tease under my breath, my lips barely moving. "If I had a whip, I'd have used it." His voice is dark silk.

I smile. I shouldn't be enjoying this. I shouldn't feel this wanted here, but I do. Not just for my body—but for what it means when I kneel for him. For what it costs me. That makes it mean more.

Drinks arrive. I sip my fruity cocktail, moaning at the sublime explosion of passionfruit and rum.

Dante's brow rises at the sound I make, then his eyes roam all over me, ownership-stamping. "You want a tour after you finish that?"

I swallow. Nod. "Yes, please, Sir."

Dark eyes flare. He nods. Pleasure explodes beneath my skin. A handful of weeks ago, I would've hysteri-sobbed into my cereal if anyone had dared to tell me those three little words would make my pussy wet.

Now they spill freely with a terrifying willingness.

The moment I drain my glass, he rises. "Come, pet."

The Gilded Cage is a cathedral of hedonism—smoke-laced air, velvet-draped alcoves, bodies in all shapes and sizes, in service, in pleasure.

I walk half a step behind Dante, my collar catching the

low light with every breath. He's calm. Controlled. But his loose hold on my wrist never leaves me.

I see thrones. Cages. A Saint Andrew's cross lit like an altar.

My heart stutters at the sight of the naked woman tied to it. Head thrown back in abject pleasure as a man wielding a whip flays her. Thighs. Breasts. Belly.

Dante leans down, voice silk and steel in my ear. "Not everything here is for you, little thief. But everything I give you will be."

The private room he chooses is all dark velvet and low lighting, the kind of place where shadows cling to the walls and secrets are expected, not hidden. A leather bench takes up the center, flanked by mounted rings, silk ropes, and mirrored panels. The glass wall on one side is tinted, but I sense we're being watched.

That's part of it.

That's part of him.

Dante closes the door behind us, locking it with a soft, metallic click. I stand where he left me, breath shallow, body already alive with nerves and want. Because I know what's coming. I asked for it. Begged for it.

And tonight, I aim to earn it.

He steps closer, circling. His eyes take in every inch of me —collared, dressed to tempt, already wet.

"You trust me, little thief?"

"Yes, Sir."

His hand lifts. Strokes down my jaw. His touch is reverent. "Good. I want them to see. I want them to know that you belong to me."

I shiver. He sees it. Smiles.

"Strip," he says softly. "Slowly. Keep your eyes on mine."

Ties. Fabric. Skin. I obey.

When I'm naked and trembling, he leads me to the bench

and bends me over it—slow, careful, like I'm precious. Because to him, I am. His to wield. His to vanquish.

He binds my wrists to the rings with crimson silk. Fastens my ankles wide. Then his hands trail up my thighs, over the plug still in place from earlier, until I whimper.

"Color."

"Green, Sir."

"Such a good submissive," he murmurs. "You're becoming everything I promised to make you."

His mouth finds my neck. My shoulder. The base of my spine. "You begged me to teach you. Look at you now."

He unfastens the plug that's become a part of my daily routine now with a twist that makes me gasp. "You're going to feel every inch of me, Dahlia."

He circles me again. Again. Trailing. Savoring. Kissing. Biting my nipples. Until slick drips down my thighs and hunger claws through my soul. "Please, Sir. Fuck me. Please."

A clack of his belt releasing. The grind of a zipper as my breath catches in anticipation. Then he's there. Poised. My Dom and desired doom.

I moan as he lines himself up—hot and hard and relentless.

Then he pushes in. Slow. Unforgiving.

"God," I cry out.

"That's right," he growls. "Take it. Take your Master's cock. Show them what you're made of. Who you were made for."

He fucks me with brutal reverence—one hand gripping my hip, the other sliding around to rub slow, wicked circles over my clit.

"You feel this?" he breathes. "This stretch, this fullness? That's me filling every inch of your greedy little body. Opening you up to who you were meant to be."

"Yes—Sir—I—Thank you."

He hisses. Grows impossibly thicker. "Again. Thank your Master again, sweet Dahlia."

Two hands on my hips, his grip cruel and steady and keeping me in the crosshairs of pleasure. "Th-thank you, Sir."

"Tell me how you feel. Tell me why you're dripping like a faucet. Tell me why this little cunt is strangling my cock like I owe it rent money?"

"Yes... no... Sir... God, please. More!"

"More of what, my little cum-slut?" His voice is a sea of gravel. "Tell me why you need more."

My vision hazes. "Because it's good. Fuck it's the best. You're the best, Sir!"

He thickens, fatter, drags his piercings over every sensitive cell. My body responds. Tightening. Slicking. Desperate for release. He knows, of course. Feels everything.

And he growls his warning. "You don't get to come yet. Not until you prove it."

"P-prove what?" I whimper.

"That you're mine. That you surrender."

He grabs a fistful of my hair, pulls me upright until my back arches, my breath ragged.

"You're doing so well," he murmurs, kissing the corner of my jaw. "You were made for this. For me."

I nod, nearly sobbing with the effort of holding back. "Please."

He rewards me with another thrust. Then another. Then stops.

"You want to come, little thief?" His voice is fire in my ear. "Then give me your eyes. Right here."

He spins me around so I'm facing him, fills my vision with him. Only him. He strokes himself slowly while watching me tremble, spread wide and wrecked.

His other hand rubs at my wet cheeks, at the tears that have fallen in his honor.

Then he pulls me close, takes my tongue with his in a filthy, sloppy kiss.

"Keep your eyes on me when you come," he says. "Don't you fucking look away."

I don't.

And when he slides back into me and gives me everything —*everything*—I shatter. Gasping, sobbing, broken open in every way.

And still, he holds me.

"Perfect," he whispers. "You're perfect."

* * *

Dahlia

I'm boneless when we return to our seat, courtesy of two more orgasms and the best aftercare in the world.

Dante starts to raise a brow when I order another cocktail, but then he stills beside me.

My heart slows. Follows his gaze. "Who's that?" I ask.

"Varric. Vesper Syndicate."

I nod. Watch him from beneath my lashes.

He sits on a raised leather throne near the back of the private lounge, surrounded by the usual leeches drawn to soiled power.

He's tall, lean in a way that's all wire and menace, like a diseased hyena dressed in Tom Ford. His black hair is slicked back with precision, but the cruel twist of his mouth pretends he's above vanity. One hand swirls a glass of something blood-red, the other strokes the thigh of the submissive kneeling beside him like she's a housecat.

Cold. Sadistic.

His name has popped up in some depraved pockets of the Dark Web. Rumor has it he's a useful appendage of Vesper—the one who handles the "messy" ends of empire. The one who makes enemies disappear. Not flashy like some of the others. Not power-hungry.

Just lethal.

He lifts his gaze. Sees us and his lip curl deepens. I'm not sure if it's a smile or a warning. Clearly, he's been waiting. And his black gaze says this is going to be fun.

"Keep those claws tucked away, pet," Dante murmurs.

"I will," I whisper. "For now."

But inside, every nerve is screaming.

Because whatever this game is, it's started.

And we just stepped onto his board.

Under the guise of taking his next sip, Dante moves closer, his body almost curving around mine. He's shielding my body with his and something cracks and melts inside me.

My fingers dance up his chest and tighten in his jacket. My own little gesture of acknowledgment and appreciation. Even though I'm primed for this fight.

"What are we—"

The lights flicker.

The music cuts.

And the collar around my throat hums—just once, a strange vibration I've never felt before.

Dante reacts instantly, grabbing my wrist. "Move," he snaps, rising. Clearly, he knows the layout of this place way better than I do because we're in a hallway in seconds, and he's pulling me back toward the emergency exit.

"What is it?" I gasp.

"Someone just activated your tag. Your collar."

"W-what? How is that even possible?" I gasp, but I know. Every damn thing under the sun is hackable. I've done more than my fair share of it. Dante doesn't respond. And I don't get to ask again, because suddenly the crowd shifts. Chaos stirs. We arrive at the exit—and Varric is there.

Not alone.

Three men block our path. And they're armed.

***

Dante

I PUSH DAHLIA BEHIND ME, already calculating. Weapons aren't allowed inside The Gilded Cage—it's one of the only rules everyone honors—but apparently the rules don't apply to everyone.

I could take my chances with the assholes, but I'm outnumbered. And the last thing I'm going to do is risk Dahlia.

Options cycle through my mind. Each discarded. And then I feel it—the chill that crawls up the back of my neck. Wrong. Something's off. A presence I didn't clock before.

I pivot fast, keeping Dahlia closer to me just as the voice cuts through the red-lit air.

"Dante."

My blood ices.

She steps forward from the shadows—heels clicking, gun steady, eyes colder than I've ever seen them.

Evelyn.

My second-in-command. My fixer. The one who's handled my dirtiest work. The woman who once joked Dahlia would be my ruin before I even knew her name.

Now she's pointing a gun at my head.

"Evelyn." My voice is stone.

She doesn't blink. "You should've let me take care of her

the night of the heist. I knew your going to get her yourself was a bad idea." Her eyes flick to Dahlia, scrutinizing her from head to toe. "She's got danger-drunk and dick-whipped written all over her, and you're stupid enough to call it what… devotion? Loyalty?"

Behind me, Dahlia stiffens. I feel the breath catch in her throat.

This is her first time hearing Evelyn's name. She doesn't know the history, but she knows betrayal when it slices close enough to bleed.

"You're with Vesper?" I demand.

"Right from the jump. They pay more than you ever will." Evelyn shrugs, but her eyes flash cold. "Loyalty doesn't pay back years of being second-best. Cleaning up your messes. Watching you obsess over one dead girl while you risk your empire over another who gets wet at the thought of ruining you." Her smile curdles and like it's a bonus, she continues. "They promised me a front-row seat when it all came crashing down."

Her eyes flick to Varric, her true boss.

He jerks his chin.

Everything happens at once.

A man lunges from the left. I elbow his throat and hear the satisfying crunch of cartilage. Another swings—a flash of steel hidden in his hand—and I drive my knee into his gut before slamming his face into the wall.

From the corner of my eye I see Evelyn take aim.

Fuck. Where's Dahlia?

She fires. The sound is deafening in the small hallway.

Dahlia screams.

Pain sears down my shoulder, hot and wet. Not lethal. Not yet.

I grab my precious submissive. No time to count the

bodies or take stock of wounds. We run. Heading outside in the empty alley will make us too easy a target.

Through the club. Through the parted crowd. Through a haze of sweat and perfume and blood.

We don't stop until we're outside, in the car, two streets away before I pull over. Her breath is choppy, her hands shaking, my coat soaked in crimson.

I press her against the wall, check her quickly for injuries. "Are you hit?"

"No," she breathes, eyes wide, stunned. "You—"

"Just a graze." I lie. "We'll get it cleaned." I feel around the collar, slide out the hair-thin microchip with hands unsteady as fuck.

She sees it—the fear I never show, the guilt twisting in my gut.

Evelyn. Vesper. The game is no longer in the dark, hiding among proxies and firewalls.

It's gone live and we're running out of bandwidth and time.

* * *

Dahlia

"She shot you," I say, voice raw.

"It's not bad." But his face says otherwise.

"Fuck, Dante—"

"We knew going in that they were dangerous," he growls, then softens. "This is what they do, Dahlia. Betray. Manipulate. Kill."

The adrenaline crashes and all that's left is the fear.

And the realization that this is real now.

No more games of dominance and surrender in silk-draped rooms.

We've stepped into a power war.

And one or both of us might perish long before our thirty days are over.

* * *

I'VE NEVER HEARD silence like this before.

Not even in the dark corners of cyberspace where I used to hide out for hours, headphones on, the world forgotten.

This silence is *thick*—the kind that sticks to your lungs and doesn't let go.

I sit on the edge of the bed in the safehouse's tiny bedroom. It's not like the penthouse—no marble, no skyline view, no decadence. Just gray walls, heavy locks, and security feeds blinking quietly from the monitor across the room.

I stare at the collar still around my throat. I didn't take it off. I thought I would. But I couldn't. Not even after the hacking scare.

Because part of me needed the weight. The reminder that even now—after a near-ambush, after blood and betrayal—I'm still tethered to him.

Even if I shouldn't be.

The bathroom door creaks open, steam curling out. Dante steps into the room, shirtless, his arm in the bandage I helped him with, torso lined with bruises and tension.

I stand without thinking.

"Let me," I whisper.

He doesn't speak. Just sits on the bed, legs wide, jaw tight. He draws me between his legs and lets me towel his hair. Apply ointment to his shoulder.

I'm gentle. He's still made of stone—but I think he's softer around me now.

"Did she mean it?" I ask finally. "Evelyn. That she wanted to watch you bleed?"

His voice is rough. "Everyone close to me eventually does."

I blink. "That's a hell of a thing to believe."

"It's not belief. It's math."

Something occurs to me. "The thirty days. It wasn't just about sex and surrender, was it?"

He stares at me, then shakes his head. "It was also about keeping my little thief safe."

"That why—"

"I nearly lost my fucking mind when you left the penthouse," he says roughly. "I thought you'd run. That they'd gotten to you first."

My mouth opens. Closes.

All this time, I thought *he* was the one keeping things from me.

But he was trying to protect me from things I didn't even know were chasing me.

I crouch between his knees. My hands on his thighs. "If this is about math, then let me be your anomaly."

That cracks him. He exhales hard. Then he cups my face. "You terrify me. You know that?"

"I know."

His forehead drops to mine. And we just breathe.

Then—"Why did the collar buzz?" I ask. "What the hell was that?"

His hand drops. He straightens.

"It's connected to Ironveil," he says. "A failsafe. Hidden in the leather. Not even Evelyn knew about it." He stops. But I know there's more. A good fucking reason.

"I'm listening."

He hesitates.

I surge closer, let him see the 'no retreat' blazing in my eyes.

* * *

Dante

"She wore one, too," I say. "My sister. A bracelet. It tracked her. So I could keep an eye on her. Keep her safe."

Dahlia stills.

"But they hacked it. Catalogued her patterns. Used my own protocol against me. Against us."

Lia's mouth tightens. "You're saying—my collar does the same. And they did the same tonight."

"I reprogrammed the chip. I swear. It was supposed to be failsafe. Ironveil is unhackable. Or so I thought. Hell, even you couldn't get in. Fuck!"

Silence. Except her breath is shaky and sharp with fear.

I look down. She swallows, and the movement shifts the collar that could very easily have ended her tonight, but her eyes don't waver from mine.

My fingers find the leather. Caress her throat. Wonder why she hasn't taken it off. Grateful that she hasn't.

"For a while, after she was gone, I hated her for not stopping when I asked her to. She wouldn't stop," I say. A reward for her continuing trust? Or an unburdening of my guilt? Who the fuck knows anymore. "Guilt drove me to pick up her crusade. To keep going."

Dahlia's eyes burn. "Then we keep going. We don't run. We finish this."

* * *

Dahlia

I DON'T EVEN REALIZE I'm climbing into his lap until I'm there —knees on either side of his hips, arms around his neck.

"No more half-truths," I whisper. "No more pushing me away."

His throat works. "This ends with them gone."

"And then what?" I ask softly, opposite of the hard, desperate push inside. "What happens to us?"

He doesn't answer. Instead, he kisses me—slow, reverent, hungry.

A kiss that says he doesn't know, but he wants to.

And that's enough.

For now.

* * *

TWO HOURS LATER...

THE MONITOR FLICKERS.

I sit cross-legged, laptop open. Dante's pacing.

"We hit them in seventy-two hours," he says. "The Gilded Cage. That's where their servers are. Buried in the basement. That's why Varric is always there. He was a stooge three years ago. Looks like he's graduated to watchdog. If we can get in there, we destroy them."

I nod. "We'll need two access points. Dual-layer breach. I can ghost my way in digitally, but we'll need a physical breach too."

"You and me," he says. "Just us." His voice **is** harsh, the spikes of betrayal sharp and deadly.

I glance up, into his face, at the arm his assistant shot at. "Because we can't trust anyone else."

"Exactly."

We stare at each other. And for the first time, there's no wall between us.

No roles. No masks. No seduction.

Just two people on the edge of war—choosing to fight *together*.

CHAPTER 16

Dahlia

Before I understood its true meaning, before I ventured onto The Club app, I thought surrender meant weakness. That giving in meant giving up control. And I've fought my whole life to keep control—over my body, my choices, my mind. But with Dante, tonight, finally... I *want* to give it away. *All the way.* Not because I've lost a fight. But because I've earned my surrender. He told me I would. I scoffed.

Now I want to weep with the weight of how right he was. Because surrendering to him doesn't feel like defeat—it feels like coming home.

He leans against the frame of the bedroom door, arms crossed, black shirt rolled to his forearms. Watching me. Assessing. Waiting to see if I'll back out. I don't. I drop to my knees on the hardwood floor without a word.

The moment I do, I feel him move. Boots silent on the mat. The click of the lock as he seals the door. A low exhale—almost like relief—as he circles me like a wolf claiming his prey. "Look at you," he murmurs, voice a rumble against the walls. "So fucking beautiful like this. Humbled. Open. Ready." My breath shudders. I'm naked except for the collar. It's become a part of me. Not a leash. Not a prison. A promise.

His fingers tangle in my hair. I don't look up. I'm the obedient, treasured little pet, eager to earn my reward. "Why are you kneeling, little thief?"

"Because I want to give you everything," I whisper. He tilts my head back. "Look at me."

I reward myself with his beautiful eyes, sharp but unreadable. "Not because you're afraid of what I'll do if you don't?"

"No, Sir."

"Not because it's part of the plan?"

"No."

"Say it."

"I'm kneeling because I trust you. I'm kneeling because you've earned it. I'm kneeling because I need to know I've earned it."

The world holds its breath.

And then he drops to his haunches in front of me. "You have no idea what that does to me." I lick my lips. Craving his. Craving everything. "Maybe… I think I do."

His hands are warm as he unfastens the collar.

"No! Wait…"

"Shhh, hush, little thief."

I hush. Heart racing. And it's just for a second. And several lifetimes. Just long enough to replace it with something heavier. A chain. Attached to his thick wrist. Oh… God. The sound of the lock echoes like thunder.

He kisses my mouth—slow and filthy, tongue stroking

mine. When he pulls back, I'm dizzy. Bliss-filled. He stands and points to the padded bench.

"Crawl."

I do. And his eyes track me every inch of the way until I reach him.

"On your back. Arms over your head."

The restraints click into place—tight but careful. Then he ties my ankles apart. Exposed. Vulnerable. *His*.

"You're so wet I can smell it," he growls, running his hand up my thigh, over my center. I arch. He doesn't touch me where I need him most. Not yet.

"I'm going to mark you," he says. "Not with ink. Not with bruises. But with *memory*. So you never forget who made you come like this."

I don't realize I'm whimpering until he smirks.

He starts with his mouth.

Dragging his tongue over my nipples. *Bite*. Down my ribs. *Graze*. To the soft skin just above my clit, where he breathes hot and slow and cruel. *Bite*.

"I'm going to tease you until you sob," he murmurs. "And then I'll wreck you so thoroughly your every code breaks and all that's left is you begging for your Master's command like a good girl."

He does exactly that.

Tongue flicking. Teeth grazing. Nipples bruised with pain and pleasure.

Fingers holding my cunt wide open as he watches every squirm and cry and filthy plea.

"Please, Sir—please—" "Please what?" he asks. "Beg properly." "Please let me come. Please destroy me."

"No."

He edges me twice. I shake. Cry.

Thrash against the cuffs.

But I don't use my safe word. Because this is pain I *want*.

When he finally stands, unbuckling his belt, his voice drops to something raw. "You're shaking. Are you scared?"

"No," I whisper. "I'm *ready*."

He prowls over me, hands on either side of my head, body bowed like an avenging god. His pierced cock rests on my pussy, just above my clit. Tapping every few seconds, reminding me of his power, his glory.

Tears stream down my temples into my hair. He licks them, watches me. Licks them.

Then, one hand—the very same attached to the chain around my neck, connecting us—fisted around his beautiful length, Dante spears me with his beautiful cock. Hilt deep. Pushing the sublime scream up, up, up my throat. When it rips, he begins. Fucking me slow at first—inch by inch until I'm split open, gasping, trembling.

He wraps his hand around my throat and says, "You want me to destroy you? Then look at me while I do."

Every thrust punches a broken sound out of me. Every squeeze around my neck makes the world spin and contract until the only thing I know is *him*.

"Who do you belong to?" he growls.

"You, Sir," I choke. "Completely."

His rhythm falters. Not with dominance. But with emotion.

"Say it again."

"You, Sir. Completely."

And I mean it. With every fucked-out breath. With every inch of me stretched to take him. Because somewhere between the bindings and the brutal honesty, I stopped fighting. Because I wanted this. Needed it.

Because for the first time in my life, being caught feels like safety.

Like maybe—just maybe—being kidnapped by Dante O'Driscoll was the best thing that ever happened to me.

Something cracks open between us. Not just my orgasm ripping through me like a scream, but the look in his eyes when he lets go and gives in to me at the same time.

"Come for me, Dahlia. Come *with* me," he commands.

I lead the only time my Master will let me. And he follows.

With my name a guttural punch gasp on his lips.

Not just as a command but as a raw *confession*.

* * *

Dante

MAYBE I SHOULDN'T HAVE DONE it. Not like that. Not when I knew it wasn't just about pleasure anymore. Not when she let me inside her in more ways than one. And yet, I couldn't stop. Because when she whispered *I trust you*, she didn't just give me power. It felt like she gave me her heart.

Wishful thinking? Fuck it. I'm not strong enough to pretend I don't want it.

I undo the cuffs gently.

She blinks up at me, dazed and spent, her thighs still trembling, lips swollen from kisses and begging. Her pussy the deep, satisfying pink flag I've accepted with every jagged edge of my black soul. I lift her into my arms and carry her to the bed like she's breakable.

Because she is. Because *I am*.

She curls into me, arms around my waist, her cheek against my chest.

"Did I please you, Sir?" she asks sleepily. I don't answer. I press my mouth to her forehead instead. Because what I want to say is *You own me.*

And that's the one truth I can't afford to speak.

Not when the thirty days are almost up.

Not when I know the moment I love her out loud… is the moment I lose her forever.

* * *

Dahlia

THIS IS IT.

The moment we've been building toward since the first crackle of electricity between us. Since that first challenge, that first kiss, that first war waged across the sheets.

I'm crouched behind a velvet panel in the upper lounge of The Gilded Cage—the Vesper Syndicate's playground—surrounded by shadows and luxury and secrets carved into the goddamn architecture.

But I'm not trembling. Not tonight. This was our only window, the night this club opens for the sleazy crème de la crème—billionaires, oligarchs, coked-up princes and oil-veined sheikhs.

My fingers are steady as I connect to the back-end of the private network, the tablet resting on my lap, my heart tuned to the familiar hum of focus.

This is my zone.

The code welcomes me like a lover.

The firewalls, trip alarms, and encrypted archives dance under my keystrokes. I'm breaking into one of the most secure systems in the digital underworld, and I'm doing it like I was born for this.

Because I was.

Somewhere downstairs, Dante is playing the role he was born to play too. Stoic billionaire. VIP member. Predator in a suit.

He's managing the floor, keeping eyes off me and securing extraction routes and overseeing the distraction crew. A masterpiece in motion.

But me?

I'm here to steal a ghost.

Dante shattered the Vesper Syndicate's soul with his previous incursions.

I'm here to ensure its heart never beats again.

That another Rina doesn't die at their hands.

Everything we've done comes down to this, except I didn't know it.

Every firewall breach, whispered command, sleepless night tangled in Dante's sheets.

Every orgasm and argument and unspoken word between us.

And I'm not doing it for vigilante justice or clicks or praise.

Not even for revenge. I'm doing it for *him*. For my mom. For the sister I'll never meet. For what they took from him. And because I've seen the man beneath the silence and the dominance—the one who keeps telling himself this ends in thirty days but touches me like I'm his salvation and his forever.

I blink back heat as the final bypass loads.

Thirty more seconds.

I whisper into the comm, "Final approach."

"Good girl," Dante's deep voice croons back in my ear. Calm. Controlled. God, I love that voice. "Update me on progress."

"Five percent left. I'm ghosting all trace logs and IP

masks. Vesper won't even know they've been scraped off the face of the earth."

A pause. Then, softer, "Be careful, little thief. Be cocky only when you're in my arms again."

My heart slams against my ribs as I press the final keystroke and watch the data flood in.

Names. Dates. Laundering routes. Assets. Victims.

Yes, S—" My breath catches when I see mine. But that's not what draws a chilling blade down my spine.

My mother's.

There, in the cold, clinical lines of Vesper's archive, is everything: her full name. Her photograph. A red-stamped classification mark: **DISPOSAL—ACQUIRED.** A timestamp from years ago. Coordinates from the hospital where she died, a victim of a vicious mugging we all knew wasn't a mugging. It wasn't twisted fate. A case of the wrong place at the wrong time.

It was them.

And not just her. My dad's name. Cross-referenced. Surveillance flagged but not activated. Meaning they were watching him too. Watching me. They've been tracking me since I was a teenager. Before college. Before hacking. Before Dante. They had a file on me. They've known for weeks.

Maybe longer. Maybe they wanted me to end up here.

"Dante," I whisper, throat tight. "They knew everything about me. About my parents."

Silence. Then, "I know," he replies, low and furious. "I suspected. Your mother's code name appeared too many times to be a coincidence."

"And you didn't tell me?"

"I didn't want to hurt you. Or scare you until we had definitive proof."

My laugh is brittle. "Too late for that."

There's a beat of silence. Then, "Get out of there, Dahlia. Now."

"I'm pulling the core archive—"

"*Now*. They know you're in there. They'll be onto you in seconds."

Fuck this. Fuck them. Ten seconds. All the time I need to take what I need and send my most lethal code.

Then I shove the drive into my boot, yank my gear into the bag, and slip out from behind the panel. The hallway's eerily quiet.

Footsteps. Not Dante's.

Shit.

I dart down the servant passage, heart hammering as I hear voices calling in a language I don't recognize. I slide the hidden panel open—straight into Dante's arms.

He grabs my face. "Are you okay?"

"I did it," I gasp, slapping the bag into his chest. "Go. Now."

We sprint for the extraction route, weaving through champagne-soaked corridors and past leather-masked patrons who have no idea the walls are bleeding.

It's only when we're in the safehouse, doors locked, drive in hand, that I let myself exhale.

###

AFTER EVERYTHING'S backed up and encrypted, Dante brings me water and pulls me into bed without a word.

We don't fuck, not this time. We just lie there, legs tangled, foreheads pressed together.

The silence says more than any dirty promise or command ever could.

Because we know. It's almost over. But I'm not broken.

Not yet.

Because for the first time in my life, there's no hollow space behind the high of why I'm doing this.

It's not for the thrill. Not for justice. Not even for the heist.

It's for *more*.

And I would do it all again.

Even knowing what's coming.

CHAPTER 17

Dahlia

The drive is encrypted, triple-locked and hidden.

Dante checked it twice after I checked it twice for tampering, trace signatures, or even ghostware embedded by Vesper. We don't want what happened with the collar to happen again.

Now we're in the bedroom, stripped down to skin and silence.

No cuffs. No masks. No roles.

Just the slow glide of his thumb along my spine as I curl into his chest.

He doesn't speak, but his body says everything. The way he holds me—like I'm precious. Like I'm breakable. Like he's afraid I'll vanish if he lets go.

I feel that too.

The weight of what we've done. What we're becoming.

The shift in us isn't loud or fireworks or declarations. It's smaller than that. Slower. The way he pulls the blanket over me like I'm the single light in his obsidian universe. The way his hand never leaves mine.

"You okay?" he asks finally, voice like gravel and night.

I start to nod, then pause. "No."

He shifts to look at me, brows furrowed.

"I'm not okay, Dante," I say, meeting his gaze. "I don't know what happens next. But I know what just happened back there. I know what I felt when I saw your face waiting for me. When I ran toward you like you were home. It… scares me."

Something in him softens, then breaks. He leans in. Kisses me like he's starving.

And then we're kissing again, slower this time. No games. Just mouths and hands and need.

I climb into his lap, straddling him. Letting him in inch by inch.

He groans, like the feel of me might undo him. "Fuck, baby," he whispers into my neck. "Dahlia. Goddess."

My heart lurches. It's the first time he's called me that.

I hold his face, eyes stinging. "You keep doing that."

"Doing what?"

"Making me slide deeper than I want to."

He grips my hips tighter. Breath shallow. "Maybe I want you to."

I ride him slowly, tenderly. Letting the ache between us melt into something sweeter. Every thrust a declaration neither of us can vocalize yet.

When I come, it's with his name against my lips like a lullaby.

And when he follows, it's with a broken sound I've never heard from him before.

Like surrender.

*   *   *

Dante

She's asleep against my chest, one hand curled against my ribs like she trusts me not to disappear.

God help me, I don't deserve this girl.

I don't deserve her laugh, her fire, the way she tears into code and danger like it's foreplay. The way she takes every part of me, even the ones I've spent years hiding.

And now I'm terrified.

Because I've given her everything. My secrets. My revenge. My soul.

I brush a kiss into her hair and whisper, "What the fuck are we doing, little thief?"

She stirs. Eyes flutter open, still hazy with sleep. "Winning."

I laugh, low and hoarse. "You think so?"

"I know so." Her voice is soft. "And when it's over, maybe I'll let you keep me."

I should tell her not to say that. Should remind her that we made a deal. Thirty days. No more.

But the words die in my throat. Because I don't want thirty days anymore.

I want *forever*.

And that scares me more than the Vesper Syndicate ever did.

*   *   *

Dahlia

. . .

The sound of Dante's breathing anchors me as I stare at the ceiling.

I can't sleep. Can't stop thinking about what we've done—what we're about to do.

One final infiltration. One last hit before we vanish for good.

His fingers are still laced with mine, even in sleep.

I turn my head to look at him. Just look.

His beautiful eyes closed, mouth slightly parted, lashes darker and longer than should be legal. He looks... at peace. Boyish, almost.

After the time I've spent with him, I know he doesn't get that often. Never lets himself rest. And maybe that's why I know something's wrong.

Because that kind of peace doesn't last long in our world. Not when people like the Vesper Syndicate are wounded but not dead.

The knock on the door is soft. Three taps.

My heart jerks.

Dante shoots up, instantly alert. "Stay here."

"Like hell I will," I whisper, already grabbing my shirt.

He's out of bed and armed in seconds, gun drawn, shoulders coiled tight as wire. I follow barefoot, adrenaline washing the sleep from my veins.

We reach the hallway together.

Another knock. Then a voice—quiet. Half-familiar.

"Mr. O'Driscoll," comes Solomon's voice. One of Dante's hackers. Trusted but verified. Repeatedly. "It's urgent."

Dante lowers the weapon but doesn't holster it. "What is it?"

Solomon doesn't look at me when he steps in. Just hands Dante a sleek tablet with shaking fingers.

"I decrypted the data. It's worse than we thought."

Dante taps the screen, scrolling rapidly. His expression sharpens with every word.

"Is that..." I step closer.

Dante nods slowly. Then exhales like the air just turned toxic.

"The basement was the tip of the iceberg," he says quietly. "From what you harvested, it looks like they're *building* something. A biometric database. Surveillance profiles. Everyone who's ever logged in, ever stepped through the doors of The Gilded Cage. Then..." He stops. Flinches.

"Dante—"

"A spiderweb of every contact, and their contact. It goes fucking on."

I step back, cold all over. "My father..."

Dante looks at me then, and there's something brutal in his stillness. Not calculation. Not strategy. Something older. Fiercer.

"I already moved him," he says, voice low. "I didn't tell you because I didn't want to spook you. But I had him pulled out the second I saw the first wave of Vesper data come in."

My knees nearly buckle with relief. "You—what?"

"He's safe. New name. Clean trail. No digital footprint. Only three people know where he is, and I'm one of them."

"Thank you, but... more secrets, Dante?"

He steps closer. Eyes locked on mine. "I swore to protect you. That includes the people you love."

The tears come fast. Hot. Messy. I swipe at them with the back of my hand, but Dante is already there, cupping my face.

"I know I've fucked up by not telling you sooner," he says, softer now. "But this part? Where safety comes first? I meant it. I'd burn the world before I let anything happen to you. Or those you love." His thumb brushes under my eye, slow and firm. "And you don't have to like every move I make, Dahlia. But you will accept that sometimes I'll act without your permission."

My breath catches. "Dante—"

"Tell me why that is, little thief."

My breath shakes my soul. "Because you're my Sir?"

His head tilts. "Is that a question?"

"You're my Sir."

"Good girl. And too fucking right."

I take a breath, scared of the upheaval. The *want*. "Why?"

His eyes burn. Sears. "Because I love you."

Bare. Raw. Powerful.

The words hit like impact trauma—no warning, no softening. My breath stutters. My lips part, but nothing comes out. Just heat behind my eyes, and the thunder of my pulse.

I wasn't ready. I didn't expect it. Not ever. But…even if a molecule dared to contemplate it—not like this. Not when we're standing in the ashes of what we thought we could control.

He watches me—like a man waiting for a verdict. Like my silence might kill him.

I step forward, just an inch. Maybe it's enough, maybe it isn't.

"I love you, Dahlia," he repeats.

* * *

Dante

SHE'S GOING to leave me.

I see it in the shift of her eyes. The way she inhales, sharp and pained. Not because she doesn't feel something—but because she *does*. Because she's brilliant enough to read between the silences. To see what I tried—and failed—to bury.

I could probably fuck her into forgetting the last five minutes. Into forgetting my love. Into obedience. But Dahlia Wynn doesn't forget. She doesn't yield unless it's on her terms.

And now I've shown her the one thing I swore never to give anyone again.

My heart.

She looks at me like she doesn't know what to do with it. Like maybe she wishes I hadn't handed it over. Like she's already halfway out the door. And maybe I should let her go. Maybe it would be the right thing. The decent thing. To release her from the danger, from me, before I pull her so far under she can't find her way back.

But I can't do it. I can't watch her walk out of my life, not when I've already imagined a thousand ways to keep her in it.

The silence between us is brutal.

Unforgiving.

The kind of silence that tears at the seams of a man already unraveling.

"I know you want to run," I say, voice raw. "Hell, maybe you *should*."

Her lips part again, but I press on.

"But I need you to understand something, Dahlia. This thing between us—it's not just sex. Not just power. Somewhere along the way, I stopped playing the game. I stopped pretending."

I look her dead in the eye. "I love you," I repeat, hoarse. "Fuck. I didn't mean to. But I do."

Her mouth opens. A beat of stunned silence.

But before she can speak—

The lights go out.

And a second later, the world *explodes*.

The blast rocks the street outside, a white-hot roar that sends us both diving to the floor as the windows blow inward and the air fills with fire and rubble.

CHAPTER 18

Dahlia

Another safehouse. Higher north. Much colder than the last. And not just in temperature—though it's nestled high in the hills, wrapped in mist and ancient stone like a tomb—but in something deeper. In the silence. The shadows. In everything we've stopped saying.

Dante hasn't spoken since we arrived.

He drove like a man possessed. Every muscle tight, every breath a fight. The bloodstains on his shirt are dry now, crusted over the ridges of his abdomen, stiff with smoke and something more brutal.

Something that doesn't wash out.

I didn't ask where we were going. I didn't ask if his hand still hurt from taking the brunt of the collapsing wall when he shoved me out of the way. I didn't ask if the security team made it out okay.

Because the look in his eyes said everything.

Because sometimes silence is the loudest fucking thing in the room.

When I flip the light switch, it flickers. Once. Twice. Then catches. The wiring is old—like everything in this place—but functional. The kitchen smells faintly of cedar and cold iron, the scent of old woodsmoke and storms clinging to the walls like ghosts.

I drop my bag on the counter. My fingers won't stop trembling.

We're alive.

Barely.

"You should shower," Dante says behind me.

His voice is hoarse. Strained. Like he's been screaming inside his own head for hours.

I nod. But I don't move.

He steps closer. Not touching and not surrounding me the way he used to—like I belonged to his orbit, like he'd rearrange the world just to keep me centered. No. He just stands there. Tense. Quiet.

Waiting for me to say something that might make this survivable.

Like he's not sure he's allowed to care anymore after he told me he loved me, *three fucking times*, and I said nothing. Because the weight of it feels like a thousand collars.

"I'll check the perimeter," he mutters, already turning.

"Dante."

He stops.

I say just that. His name. But it vibrates through the space between us like a bomb ticking down. I don't even know what I want to say.

My throat is thick with unshed screams. With rabid need. With questions I don't know if I want the answers to.

Will we make it?

Do you want to keep me?

Will you stop me from being who I want to be?

Instead, I ask, "Did we lose anyone?"

A pause. A breath.

"Not yet," he says.

And the silence that follows feels like death.

When the door shuts behind him, I finally let myself cry.

Not the angry, hot tears that come from fear or pain. The kind that seep out slow. That leave you hollow.

I sink to the floor, curled in on myself, and cry into my knees like I did the night my mother died.

Because this uncertainty. This loss? I only felt like this when she was taken from me.

And yet, Dante's alive. He told me he loves me.

So why do I feel like I'm grieving anyway?

* * *

Dante

THERE'S a special kind of irony to swearing you'll keep the woman you love safe... seconds before the world shatters around her.

I walk the perimeter twice. Maybe three times. I've lost count.

The sensors are clear. The drones we hacked show no signs of pursuit. The safehouse is tight. Secure.

None of it matters.

Because I can't go inside. Not yet. Not while the scent of her skin is still in my lungs and I'm still shaking from the thought of losing her.

She almost died.

I watched that fireball ignite in the dark and *knew*—just

knew—it would swallow her whole if I didn't move fast enough. I don't even remember dragging her down, pressing my body over hers, taking the burn.

But I remember her voice.

"Are you okay?"

Not *Am I okay?* Not *What the fuck just happened?*

She asked about *me*.

That this thing between us was supposed to be about the contract. The heist. The control.

It was. It is. But…

Fuck.

Am I the asshole for dwelling on what I'll do if she doesn't love me back? How even now I flirt with a different heist. A kidnapping. The forever kind. I have the means to take what I don't deserve.

No fucking doubt.

But I've never *wanted* anything this badly. Not vengeance. Not victory. Just her. Her laugh and her chaos, her trust in my hands. And maybe it's selfish, dropping my guard and daring her to break the only thing that's still mine—a black, charred heart—at her feet in the middle of a fucking war… but I don't care. Because if she walks away now…

Fucking Christ, she won't get far.

And those chains sitting at the bottom of my go-bag?

She'll wear them knowing she's the only goddamn thing keeping me from going under.

* * *

WHEN I FINALLY GO BACK INSIDE, SHE'S curled in the armchair, knees drawn up, one of my shirts wrapped around her small, curvy body like armor. She looks breakable. Not fragile. *Dangerously breakable.* Like one more wrong move will be the final straw.

Her laptop glows faintly in her lap. Fingers tapping in code. Fast. Focused.

"I'm running a new backdoor," she says without looking up. "We'll have one shot at this. I'll burn through the last layer if I brute-force it."

Her voice is cold. Calm. Clinical.

But I hear it.

I *feel* it.

The distance she's building brick by fucking brick.

I move to the kitchen, pour two drinks. Bourbon. Neat. My hand trembles just slightly as I set hers down on the side table.

She doesn't touch it. Just types as we hurtle toward the crossroads.

I could lie again. Stay in character. The cold, ruthless bastard who got her into this mess and will see her through the end of it.

Or I could sit and finally face this silent war head-on.

I sit. And I say it. "I never wanted it to go this far." My voice cracks. Raw. "Not with you."

She turns, eyes wide, watchful. Is her breath held? "Where was the end point, Dante? With me bound and gagged at the back of your car? On my way to a landfill or back in my apartment?"

My laugh is coarse, searing. "The latter. Hopefully."

Her eyes pierce mine. And yes, her breath is definitely held. In hope. Or rejection?

"Hopefully," I repeat, softer this time. "But you have a habit of getting under skin that's supposed to be bulletproof."

A beat.

I should say it again. *I love you.* I should take the risk. Strip it bare like I stripped her body and asked her to trust me to Master it.

But I don't. *Fucking pussy.*

Instead, I lean back in the chair and tip my glass to my lips. "Anyway. You're still here. Which means I didn't fuck up as badly as I thought."

I offer a crooked smile. Deflection, laced in charm. A joke wrapped in panic.

Her lips part slightly. Like she wants to say something. Like she knows what I didn't say. But she closes them again.

And the silence between us sharpens.

I let it hang there.

Because the truth is, I'm terrified—*not* of the Vesper Syndicate, not of losing the mission.

I'm terrified of losing *her*.

So I stay silent.

And I pray she doesn't see through it. Doesn't see the chains silently unfurling. Ready to capture and keep what might not be mine.

***

Dahlia

THE CODE BLURS.

My fingers hover over the keyboard, the screen glowing with lines I can't focus on. The digits and backdoors and security tunnels—none of it matters right now.

Not when I can still feel the ghost of Dante's touch and silence, even when he's across the room.

He sits by the fire now. Not close enough to burn, but close enough to feel the heat. One leg sprawled out, his elbows on his knees, head bowed like he's bearing some invisible weight. Like if he looks up, the world might crack open and swallow us both.

I close the laptop slowly. Swallow hard.

"You're doing that thing again," I say softly.

His gaze lifts. Charcoal-grey eyes like a storm held behind glass. "What thing?"

"The silence thing. The blaming yourself thing."

A beat.

"Isn't that what ended us here? Another fucking safehouse?"

My heart squeezes. "You can't take the world on your back and pretend I don't get to choose. Not for Rina. Not for me."

His eyes narrow. Probe. "I didn't choose for you to almost die."

"You didn't choose to love me either, I think."

Fuck. Not what I was going to say.

The words hang there. Heavy. Awful.

True.

Dante flinches, just slightly. His hand flexes against his thigh, like he wants to reach for me but doesn't trust himself to. Or worse—doesn't trust me to want him anymore.

I rise from the armchair and cross the room, slow and quiet. Bare feet on the old wood floor, wearing nothing but his shirt, like it still matters whose skin it touched last.

When I stop in front of him, I don't speak. I lower to my knees instead. My favorite place.

He exhales like I've hit him. Not with force. With mercy.

"You shouldn't be down there," he says, but he doesn't stop me.

"I want to be."

He brushes a hand through my hair, fingertips skimming my cheek. "You scared the fuck out of me with that close fucking shave. Again."

I nod, my throat tight. "You scared me too."

His voice turns ragged. "When I thought I lost you—"

"You didn't."

"Not yet."

The crack splits open.

And I fall in.

"I used to wonder," I whisper, "what my dad would say if he saw me like this. If he knew I was halfway in love with a man like you. A man who breaks the rules for a living but for the wrong team. Who might not make it out the way Mom didn't."

Dante doesn't move. Doesn't breathe.

"I think if he pulled himself out of his misery long enough, he'd hate it," I go on, soft and bitter. "And even if I told him I discovered I was wrong, that you were on my kind of righteous crusade, I think he'd still say I'm repeating history. My mom died chasing something she thought mattered. Maybe I'm doing the same."

"He may be right about me, but you're not her," he says, low and fierce. "No," I agree. "But I love like her. Fast. All in. Firewalls all the way down."

I slide my hand over his knee, up his thigh, until my palm rests over his heart. His pulse is erratic beneath it. Strong. Real. Terrified.

"I know what this was supposed to be," I whisper. "Thirty days. A game. Control and obedience."

"Dahlia..."

"But it's not that anymore, is it?"

He doesn't answer. Because we both know the truth.

When his hands finally touch me, they tremble. His fingers trail over my waist, up my spine, then fist the back of my shirt as he pulls me forward into his lap.

Our mouths meet with a desperation we've been choking on for days.

This isn't like the other times.

This is deeper. Slower. More savage in its softness.

His tongue slides against mine with reverence, like he's memorizing every taste. His hands explore with reverent greed, pulling the shirt over my head, exposing me to firelight and his gaze.

"You're still mine," he growls, voice hoarse. "Even if it kills me."

I straddle him. Cup his jaw. "Then show me."

He lifts me effortlessly and lays me on the rug in front of the fire.

And he does.

He shows me how much he needs me—with every kiss, every thrust, every command whispered into my open mouth. He doesn't fuck me like a dominant staking a claim.

He makes love to me like a man unraveling.

When I come, it's with his name breaking on my lips and his body buried deep inside mine. My tears wet his cheek as he leans his forehead against mine.

"I want more than thirty days," he whispers.

His hands clench on my hips.

"Then take it," I say. "Take everything."

We lie there, tangled in sweat and silence.

And for a moment, it feels like we're not running anymore.

Just surviving. Together.

* * *

Dante

SHE'S asleep on my chest, her favorite place to be with one arm slung across my stomach. Her breath warm against my skin. Her leg hooks over mine like she never plans to let go.

Like this... *us*... was always inevitable.

I smile in the dark as my palm moves slowly over the bare skin of her back. Tracing the soft curve of her spine.

Savoring the weight of her, the silence between us, the fire crackling low and golden nearby.

I've never known this kind of peace. Not once.

Not in the years before the Syndicate. Not in the years after.

And certainly not since Ironveil began swallowing every piece of me I didn't already burn.

But she's here. Curled against me like I'm her home. And for the first time in my goddamn life, I think about what it might mean to be someone else.

Not the man with all the secrets. Not the monster hunting bigger monsters with a target on his back. Just... hers.

Dahlia shifts, breath catching. Then her fingers curl into my side like a kitten clawing for reassurance. She doesn't open her eyes, doesn't speak. But she *feels* me.

The knowing in her touch undoes me.

I dip my chin and kiss the top of her head. Despite her shower earlier, she smells like sweat and ash and me.

"You're not sleeping," she murmurs.

"Neither are you."

Her lashes flutter open. Her eyes are dark and storm-lit in the low light. "Too much in my head."

"About what?"

A pause.

"You. Me. This."

My chest tightens. The chains rattle. "Tell me," I say quietly. "Even if it's fucked up." Even if it gets you shackled and bound to me while I figure out ways to steal the heart that's not yet mine.

She props herself up on her elbow, fingers trailing down my chest. "It's not fucked up. That's the problem."

My brows lift.

"I thought you'd be a one-night mistake," she says, a crooked smile tugging at her lips. "Or a thirty-day one. That I'd pay up, gather info, get the hell out. And maybe... okay, most definitely, rob you again."

I smirk in the dark. "And now?"

"The world's not ready for the things I want to do to keep you mine." My breath leaves me in a rush.

Fuck.

She doesn't blink. Doesn't flinch. Just stares at me like she's laying her soul bare and waiting for me to do the same.

"You scare me," I admit.

She nods. Somber and divine. "You said that before."

"I know. Still true. Truer."

Her lips tremble. Just slightly. "I'm terrified too, if it helps. With how much I want to make it real."

"Dahlia..." I exhale roughly. "I fucking love you. But..." My throat works. I cover her hand with mine, anchoring us there. Just that simple press of flesh to flesh. "I don't know how to do this any other way than owning you—body, mind, heart. Controlling every inch, code and component until you forget who you were before me. I will take you apart, remake you, and never give you back. Do you understand?"

"I understand, Sir."

"Then take a beat before you jump. One way or another."

She nods. "Okay. I will."

God. She makes it sound so simple.

And somehow, impossibly, I believe her.

Because I've already given her things I've never given anyone—my trust, my pain, my complete Dominance. She's tasted every bitter part of me and still looks at me like I'm something worth keeping.

And yet she hasn't said the words. Maybe she's hedging. Giving herself an out?

Maybe this is just the start of everything falling apart.

Or maybe it's the moment we build something neither of us planned for.

She leans in and kisses me again. No heat this time. Just warmth and lips on lips. A kind of promise.

I pull her back into my arms, wrapping her tightly against me, and we fall asleep like that.

Tangled.

Surrendered.

Together.

For now.

CHAPTER 19

Dahlia

The quiet of the safehouse is deceptive. It's the kind that doesn't lull you—it hums with the climb to a crescendo. Whether it'll be catastrophic or sublime? I have no fucking idea.

I sit on the floor beside the low table, legs folded, laptop open. The glow from the screen lights up my face.

Dante's asleep in the other room. Or pretending to be. I can feel the tension in the walls, the way silence sharpens when we're no longer touching.

I log into the chat server under my old alias. The one that used to make me feel untouchable. Invincible.

I need that tonight.

Three seconds and the screen floods with notifications.

ByteQueen: holy shit
ByteQueen: is that really you??
Zero_Day: you've been ghost for weeks!

Ghostfox: you alive or what? We been played?

FangsOut: What happened, Spec? Tell me you didn't get got by Triple D???!

I bite my lip. The words hit harder than they should.

ByteQueen: you ok?

FangsOut: if he's keeping you prisoner blink twice

Zero_Day: or hack the Vatican again

Ghostfox: or break something beautiful. You always were best at that.

That one makes me pause.

Break something beautiful.

I inhale, fingers poised over the keys.

Not dead. Not fine either.

Thinking about one last stand.

A flurry of replies flood in.

Zero_Day: hell yes

ByteQueen: you mean it??

FangsOut: go big or go ghost, baby

Whiteout: what do you mean one last stand tho?

Ghostfox: make it hurt. Make it worth it.

I stare at that last one.

Make it worth it.

Make him *worth it.*

He loved me in a language of violence and control, but he also held me like I was holy. And I let him. I let him in deeper than anyone ever has.

I close the chat, fingers trembling.

And now I'm on the edge of a precipice. My fingers trace the edge of the collar. Back and forth. Back and forth. Then for the first time since Dante put it on me, I finger the clasp.

The sharp exhale drives my gaze to the bedroom door.

My thumb freezes on the clasp. I'm suddenly aware of every breath, every beat of my heart echoing inside the collar he gave me.

The dark doorframe hides most of Dante's bulk, but the voice—low, dark, velvet wrapped in iron—fills the room as his hand settles on the jamb.

A single brow lifts, as if he's offered me a dare wrapped in silk and razor-wire. "You thinking of taking it off, little thief? Stealing away when I'm not looking?"

I swallow. God, the way my whole body betrays me just by hearing him.

"Maybe," I answer. *Translation: yes, but only because I'm terrified.* "You said you loved me in the middle of a cyber-attack, when the sky's servers maxed at Cat-5. I'm still not sure whether I've survived the blast or not."

He strolls closer, sealing us inside a bubble of tension and possibility. Even sleep and sex-ruffled, he radiates authority. Each measured stride shortens my breath.

"Would you like me to start again? Go slower?" he says, voice rough. "Beg?"

The admission shocks me.

Dante O'Driscoll doesn't beg. He shatters empires.

His mouth curves as he fingers the collar's clasp, never breaking eye contact. He could open it in a second, but he doesn't.

Instead, he presses the metal to my pulse. *Do you feel how fast you're racing for me?* the gesture says.

"For weeks," he murmurs, "I've asked for pieces—your obedience, your risk, your pleasure. Tonight I want the only thing you keep behind firewalls even I can't breach." A breath. "Tell me, Dahlia." A rough plea lurks behind alpha dominance.

"What if I don't know how to say it?"

"Then bleed it out in any language you have left."

He cups my jaw, thumb stroking the hinge until the trembling eases. His touch is neither gentle nor harsh; it's *anchoring.* He drops to one knee, bringing that formidable height level with mine. It undoes me more than any order.

"Collar or no collar," he says, "you stay because you *choose* me. Or you try to walk away when this is over."

"*Try?*"

"I refer you to everything I said last night? With the addendum that I will try to let you go." A muscle jumps along his jaw. "It would kill me. But I'd do it. The only thing I can't guarantee is long-term success of keeping that promise."

That's the difference between a captor and a Dom who loves. It cracks something wide open in a heart.

I close my fingers around his wrist. "Say it again. Help me with this."

His eyes turn molten. "I love you, Dahlia. Nothing you do or say will change that—only what I do to protect it. To earn yours."

"And if it shatters me?"

He smiles—a sliver of pain and awe. "Then I'll learn how to hold broken things without cutting myself."

My vision blurs. The room swims. For the first time since the collar snapped shut, I *want* to remove it—only so I can hand it back, a gift instead of a shackle. My fingers slide to the clasp.

His hand covers mine. "Your choice," he says.

Three syllables that sound like *forever*.

I unhook the metal, set it in his palm. The air feels shockingly cool on my neck. Naked. Frantic. Vulnerable.

"Put it back on me," I whisper, "only if you believe I can be your equal *and* your submissive."

His eyes flare. He rises, towering, and circles behind me. The collar clicks in place—no longer a claim of possession, but of promise. A kiss where the clasp meets my skin.

"Look at me, little thief."

I turn. He lowers to my height again, forehead touching mine.

"I'm not running," I say, voice trembling but sure. "I'm scared I'll never measure up. That loving you means losing myself. But the truth?" I swallow. "I came alive in the dark with you. I want every impossible piece—field ops, playrooms, boardrooms, coffins if we must."

I draw a shaky breath. "I love you, Dante. And I love and hate how much it hurts."

His laugh is wet, shaky. "You're the only pain that feels like oxygen and salvation."

He moves before I can think—grabs my wrists, yanks me into him, mouths crashing together like we've both been starved. A rough kiss—salted by tears, tempered by steel—seals confession into covenant. He pulls back just enough to speak.

"On your knees," he orders softly. "Where my love belongs."

I kneel, not in defeat but devotion. He unfastens a silk leash from his pocket, clips it to the collar, and presses it into my hands.

"You hold it," he says. "Power goes both ways."

I clutch the silk, breathless. The symbolism wrecks me more than any flogger.

"Safe word?" he prompts.

"Killshot."

"Color?"

"Emerald." The strongest green there is.

"Then listen carefully." He straightens, voice sliding into command. "Tonight you'll hold my gaze while I have your heart, and you'll come when I grant it—so hard you'll forget how fear tastes."

Heat spirals low and vicious. "Yes, Sir."

His answering groan is reverent. He leads me out of the

living room. Back to our bed. "Up on the bed, wrists to the headboard. I want you open so I can write devotion in sweat."

The mattress dips under his weight; leather buckles secure me in place, not unkind but unbreakable. He strips, every exposed inch surrendered to the slow roll of muscle and intent. Moonlight paints his torso in silver, the ink on his ribs a map of battles won and wounds endured.

He kneels between my spread thighs, eyes locked on mine. "Breathe," he reminds, and I realize I haven't.

Air rushes in—followed by his mouth on my inner knee, the inside of my thigh, higher, higher.

He pauses at my needy pussy, hot breath teasing slick heat.

"I promised complete surrender," he murmurs. "You've earned it."

His tongue flicks. My spine bows. "Sir—"

"Eyes on me," he orders. "Show me forever."

Every flick, every press, every slow thrust of fingers is a syllable in a love letter only we can read. Pleasure climbs, coils, threatens, and tears sting my eyes.

He holds my gaze, an anchor in a storm.

"Let go," he says—a decree and an absolution.

I shatter—loud, violent, free. He doesn't look away, even as my cries break the ceiling open. Only when the tremors ease does he surge up, kissing the tears from my cheeks.

He frees my wrists, but I stay clinging.

We breathe each other in, and he fills me, slow and steady. And when he bottoms out, his cock rooted deep, deeper than he's ever been, my Dom doesn't move.

I love you. On a loop. That's all I need. All we need.

We shatter again, our firewalls decimated, leaving us weak and bare and bliss-drenched.

"Dante?" I whisper, trembling laughter threading the ruin.

"Yes, little thief?"

"Thank you for finding me."

His smile is soft power, wrapped in steely intent. "You were never lost—just waiting to be stolen correctly."

We curl into each other, sweat cooling, hearts syncing.

Outside, the war still waits.

But inside this orbit, we've already won.

* * *

Dahlia

THE MOMENT the encrypted drive slides into place and the last firewall crumbles, the world holds its breath.

Then—silence.

Not static or system noise. Not Dante's curse when a timer hits zero. Just the pure, ringing hush of a clean break. A closed loop. A heist finished.

It's over.

The Vesper Syndicate's vault is gutted. Every offshore account, every blackmail file, every veiled threat catalogued, cracked open like a skull at our feet.

I don't move until Dante locks the server room at Obsidian behind us, the scene of my tenth heist and his final one.

No fanfare or live-streaming or witnesses.

Just Dante and me, bleeding adrenaline, soaked in a high that tastes like ash and triumph.

It's only once we're in the car, coasting in the dark, that I realize I'm crying. Quiet, steady tears that streak my cheeks and soak the collar still fastened tight around my throat.

Not from fear. Not even from the rush.

Relief.

A full-body, bone-deep surrender to the fact that we made it out.

That the data I ripped from Vesper's marrow finally lays my mother's ghost to rest—and, in the same breath, slays the monsters I've been fighting in her name.

His hand finds mine across the console. Rough and shaking. Holding tighter than I expect.

"You did it," he says, voice broken and reverent.

"We did," I whisper.

I squeeze his hand back. And don't let go.

* * *

Dante

THERE ARE no words when we reach the penthouse.

Only the pounding of our hearts. The echo of destruction still thundering in our blood. I strip out of my gear in the hall.

She moves beside me, silent and fluid. Still riding the high.

I watch her.

Her boots come off first. Then the utility belt, unbuckled with one flick of those thief-trained fingers. She peels off her body armor, layer by layer, until only the collar remains.

And then she turns.

Dark blue eyes—haunted and blazing. Full lips swollen from the stress-bite she always gives herself when she's deep in code.

"Master," she says. Then, "Fuck me."

She says it like a command.

Like a plea. Like something holy.

And I'm undone.

I lift her—because kneeling would be too small for this moment.

I carry her into the playroom like she's fire and salvation all at once. My arms full of the only thing I've ever truly wanted to protect.

I don't speak as I strip the last of her clothing away. Don't order her. Don't bind her.

Not yet.

Tonight isn't about ownership.

It's about worship.

* * *

Dahlia

THE STRAPS of the leather swing are cool beneath my skin.

Familiar.

But tonight, there's no edge to it. No punishment in the air.

Just him. His hands and his mouth.

Every stroke is reverent. Every kiss a thank you and a warning and a benediction all rolled into one. His fingers trail down my spine, slow and aching.

They pause at the plug he insisted I wear through the heist, keeping me *his* even in enemy territory.

He leans in, breath hot against my ear.

"You were perfect," he murmurs. "So fucking perfect. And mine."

The words crash through me, making my breath stutter.

I nod. I tremble. I *feel*.

"I love you, Sir. Yours. Always. Completely," I whisper. And I mean it.

He binds my wrists high—not tight. Just enough. Just so I know it's real.

The soft leather cuffs wrap around me like vows.

Then he takes up the flogger.

Not to punish but to bless.

* * *

Dante

I TOUCH HER LIKE A PRAYER. Like she's something holy.

Something I have no business kneeling before—but do anyway.

She's bound, but not to break. Her wrists hang above her, soft and willing, cuffs snug but not cruel. I watch her body—lush, trembling, flushed with heat and high from the win—as she melts beneath every inch of my focus. Her dark hair spills down her back, damp with sweat. Her breath is shallow, but steady. Expectant.

The flogger falls in a gentle rhythm, leather whispering across the curve of her ass, the backs of her thighs, her calves. A hairsbreadth from her slick and shining pussy.

No pain—just the bite of sensation. The gift of presence.

Her moans come softly at first, then louder as her body sways into it, surrendering deeper with every stroke.

She spreads her thighs wider without being told.

She *knows* what's next.

And so do I.

But I don't rush.

I drop to my knees behind her, between her splayed legs. I

press my mouth to the skin just above the plug keeping her open for me—claiming her again, reminding her she's still mine. Then lower.

I kiss the inside of her thighs, nipping, teasing, tasting the sweat and surrender there until she's *sobbing*, gasping out half-formed pleas.

Then I lick her.

Soft and slow at first. Then deeper. Then *crueler*.

I edge her once, twice, a third time—until her body is thrumming, her voice wrecked and hoarse. Her safe word dances behind her teeth, but she never says it.

Because she *trusts* me.

Because she *wants* this.

Because she knows I'll never take her further than she can go—but I'll damn well take her to the edge.

When I finally rise, I drag my cock over her slick folds, teasing her entrance, rubbing metal against skin, feeling her tremble. The way she arches. The way she gasps. Begs.

I push inside her ass. *Slow.*

Deep.

Possessive.

Heaven.

My cock sinks into her inch by inch, and I swear—God help me—I feel it in my soul. She's tight and wet and clutching at me like she needs this as badly as I do. Like she's taking me in *everywhere*—mind, body, fucking soul.

She throws her head back, dark blue eyes glassy with need.

"Say it," I growl, one hand curving gently around her throat—take her breath just enough to make her feel it. "Say you're mine."

Her whole body clenches as she cries out, *"I'm yours. Always."*

It flays me.

The sound of her. The feel of her. The way her body opens for me, bare and fearless and *mine*.

I thrust harder, deeper, unable to hold back the growl that rips from my chest. My control frays with every stroke. I feel her clench around me, hear her whimper and gasp, her pleasure building again like a wave.

I press my forehead to hers, our breaths tangled and labored. My thrusts slow—not out of mercy, but awe. Reverence.

"And I'm yours," I whisper, barely able to speak. "God help me, Specter. I've *always* been yours."

* * *

Dahlia

When I come, it's with his name torn from my throat like truth.

My body convulses around him, every nerve lit like the last star in a dying sky. His cock throbs inside me, buried so deep I don't know where he ends and I begin. And for a long, suspended moment, he doesn't move.

He just holds me.

Like I'm the only thing in this fucked-up world he can't rebuild if it got damaged.

Like letting go might break him more than it breaks me.

His breath shudders out. His arms tremble around my hips, his forehead pressed against mine like a prayer, or maybe a promise.

I lift my bound wrists. I mean to touch his jaw. To anchor us both. But he leans in first and kisses the inside of my elbow. Soft. Gentle. Like it's sacred.

Like *I* am.

Neither of us says anything for a long while. We don't need to.

Eventually, he unbinds me with fingers that linger too long on every strap. Then he lifts me, carries me to bed like the end of a ritual, and tucks me against him as if sleep were safety, as if the world could wait.

We curl together like we're learning each other all over again.

His breath at my temple.

My hand splayed over his chest.

No more contracts. No more commands.

Just this. Just us.

And for the first time in my life, I don't dream of loss and guilt and ghosts.

I dream of *forever*.

EPILOGUE

Dahlia

One Year Later

STEAM CURLS around us like juicy secrets and silk.

I'm perched on the edge of the counter in nothing but one of his shirts—white, crisp, smelling like him. Dante's fresh out of the shower, towel slung low on his hips, hair wet and mussed. Ridiculously handsome. Unfairly smug.

I tilt my head, watching him in the mirror as he runs a hand through his hair, those dark eyes tracking my reflection like a target. He's so used to being the one in control. So used to watching me fall apart.

Not tonight.

"Something on your mind, little thief?" he asks, his voice warm with amusement.

I smile slowly. "Yeah. You."

Then I stretch—just a little—and let the shirt ride up high on my thighs. I don't miss the way his gaze drops, darkens. How his fingers flex like he's already imagining them on my skin.

I hook a finger at the collar of the shirt. "You know, I've been thinking…"

"Dangerous," he murmurs, stepping closer.

I let him.

Until he's right between my knees, hands braced on either side of me. But before he can kiss me, I smirk and whisper, "You're awfully tall for someone so easy to topple by someone so *little*."

He stills.

"What?" he breathes, almost disbelieving.

I lean in, brush my lips over his jaw. "I mean, for someone so big and bad, you really let *little* ole me wreck you."

His hand fists in the hem of the shirt. His voice is gravel. "Is this you paying me back for calling you little, baby?"

I look up at him through my lashes. Grip the cock tenting his towel. Stroke stroke stroke. "Maybe. Just a *little*."

He groans like he's in pain. "Careful, Dahlia. Payback might just backfire on you."

I grin, impossibly smug. "Has that ever stopped me, Master?"

Five minutes. That's all it takes to topple my Dom when I take him down my throat.

"Jesus! Fuck! That was…incredible."

Yup.

I fucking win.

Next Day

. . .

I'M NAKED.

Except for the plug snug inside me—polished obsidian, rimmed with rose gold—and the digital interface flickering across the table like it's just another lazy Saturday morning.

Dante's hand rests against the back of my neck. Warm and steady and possessive in the way only he knows how to be. His thumb brushes my skin in slow, idle circles, like he's reminding me I belong to him—that he belongs to me, too.

I'm half-curled in the big leather chair of our upstairs lounge, one foot tucked under me, a stylus dangling from my teeth while I tap through firewall overlays and biometric backdoors like I'm shopping for shoes.

Three tabs are open—each one tied to a potential entry strategy—and our audience is already casting their votes.

It's become a bit of a tradition.

One year since we burned Vesper to the ground, and now we're semi-retired... sort of. Just the occasional job. For the right cause. The right thrill.

And tonight?

Tonight's a good one.

"Oh look," I chirp, shifting slightly so the plug presses deeper, making me squirm. "Option C is winning by a landslide."

Dante's gaze doesn't flick to the screen. His focus stays glued to me. It always does. "Option C is a death trap," he says mildly.

"Which means...?" I glance at him out of the corner of my eye.

He smirks. "So obviously, you're going to do it."

I flash him a grin. "What can I say? Our followers have excellent taste in mayhem."

He leans down, mouth brushing the shell of my ear, his voice rough with promise. "If you make it back without a scratch," he murmurs, "I'll fuck your ass so hard you won't be able to sit for a week."

My breath catches like it always does when he talks like that—casual filth in that velvet-dark voice that makes my thighs clench and my brain short-circuit.

God, I love this man.

I pretend to ponder. "Hmm. So what you're saying is... I *shouldn't* sabotage the escape route to spice things up?"

His hand tightens slightly at my nape in warning. "Dahlia."

"Fine, fine." I wave him off playfully, tapping through another encrypted node. "I'll behave. Ish."

He sinks down onto the ottoman in front of me, still shirtless from this morning's workout, the scars across his chest catching the light like runes of power and blood. His eyes lock on mine with that look—half amusement, half menace, all Dante.

"You're insatiable," he says softly. "And reckless. And mine. So absolutely no scratches."

I shiver. Not from fear. Never from fear.

From *belonging*.

"Always," I whisper, leaning forward to press a kiss to his mouth—quick and dirty and hot enough to promise later.

His hand trails down my spine, stopping at the plug. His thumb taps the base lightly.

"You want that reward?"

I arch my brow. "What do you think?"

He groans under his breath. "Then win for me, little thief."

My grin is wicked. "Now I *have* to."

THIRTY MINUTES Later

. . .

GETTING DRESSED in front of Dante is a game. A tease. A ritual.

He sits back on the edge of the bed, shirt unbuttoned, tie hanging loose, eyes devouring every movement like I'm the only show in town.

Which, to him, I probably am.

I hook the thigh holsters first, the leather hugging my curves like a second skin. Then the sheer black mesh blouse, the one that's more suggestion than coverage. My cropped jacket hugs my waist, the hem brushing just above the waistband of my tight skirt.

He watches me clip a slim blade to my boot, then pin my hair up, twisting it high to reveal the diamond collar glittering at my throat.

A symbol. A promise. A challenge.

"Color?" he asks as he finally starts to button his shirt, one slow movement at a time.

I smirk into the mirror, eyes locking with his. "Green." Then I blow him a kiss over my shoulder and add, "Greedy little green goddess, Daddy."

The growl he lets out is instant. Low. Dangerous.

"Keep talking like that," he warns, sliding his cufflinks into place, "and I'll fuck you in the alley before we even make it to the vault. You'll heist with cum dripping down your thighs."

I bite my bottom lip, humming like I'm tempted.

And God, I *am*.

But I want the whole show tonight. The full reward. The high of a job pulled off perfectly—*then* the bliss of being undone.

So I wink. "Later."

* * *

We make it in and out with barely a hitch.

The tech was older than expected.

The building's vault wasn't even triple firewalled. The guards were glorified bouncers with tasers and bad attitudes. It was almost too easy.

But the *thrill*? That was still very real.

The way we moved together—fluid, sharp, seamless. His hands covering me as I pried open the last sequence. His mouth at my ear counting down the final seconds. My fingers feeding him the drive, heart pounding.

Our shadows slipping into the night like vapor.

And when we burst into the penthouse, the door slamming shut behind us, the only thing louder than the alarms in my blood is the sound of our laughter.

Dante locks the door. I'm already kicking off my heels. Unzipping my skirt. Peeling off the sheer blouse and jacket like I'm shedding skin.

"Was I good?" I ask, backing toward the playroom, my collar catching the light like a gleaming promise, skirt around my thighs.

He doesn't answer with words.

He *stalks*.

All that predator energy still coiled tight from the job, now zeroed in on me. His tie still hanging loose. His sleeves rolled up. His eyes locked on my dripping heat between my thighs.

"You were fucking *brilliant*," he growls.

He catches me before I can reach the mat, yanks me flush against him, then spins me, bending me over the padded edge like I'm a gift he's waited *all night* to unwrap.

The spreader bars keep my legs wide open.

The plug pops free with a slick, obscene sound, and I whimper as cool air teases my sphincter. My knees wobble. My pussy clenches.

I'm so wet I can feel it dripping down my thighs.

Dante groans behind me. "You came from the thrill, didn't you?"

I can't lie to him. Not when his fingers stroke through my soaked folds, not when one slides inside me like it knows *exactly* where I ache.

"Maybe," I breathe. "Or maybe I just really wanted my reward."

* * *

Dante

She gasps when I push in.

Tight.

So tight. So fucking sublime.

My cock stretches her inch by inch, the resistance divine, her body trembling against mine as I fill her slowly—carefully. But not too carefully. She wants the stretch. Craves the pressure. Has begged for it, over and over, until I promised her this.

"God, you were made for this," I rasp, my grip iron around her hips. My fingers bruise with reverence. My control barely holding. "This ass... fuck, baby. You love giving me this part of you, don't you?"

"Yes, Sir," she breathes, and her voice breaks on the words.

That sound.

That surrender.

It goes straight to my chest like a detonation. A soul-deep quake.

"You love being my good little thief." I slam in deeper,

groaning at how her body strangles my cock, at how perfectly she *yields*.

She whimpers. Just a little.

And it shatters me.

Because she's everything—this wild, brilliant, impossible woman who crawled under my skin like a drug and *stayed*. Who turned my world inside out and then rebuilt it, better and more beautiful than I ever deserved.

I wrap her hair around my fist, drag her upright until her spine curves against my chest. Her head lolls to the side, exposing the diamond-studded collar at her throat. I kiss it. Bite it.

"Know what I'm going to do," I growl into her ear, "after I make you come?"

She moans, needy, breathless. "What?"

"Put a ring on your finger."

She freezes.

"My last name on your tongue," I continue, slower now, fucking her deep and mean. "Maybe a new collar too. Gold this time. And then I'll do this again. And again. Every fucking day if I have to."

She lets out a trembling laugh—then it breaks, crashes into a soft sob of pleasure as I angle my thrusts just right.

"You're never letting me go," she whispers, voice splintering with feeling.

"Damn right I'm not. Now come for your Master."

I hold her through it.

Through the wave that overtakes her. Through the shaking sobs and stuttering moans and the way her body milks me, tight as a vice, her orgasm wracking her completely.

I keep fucking her through it, slower now, claiming every inch of her. Letting her cry. Letting her *feel* everything I've been too fucked up to say until now.

She's never been more mine than in this moment.
And I've never been more hers.

* * *

SHE'S BACK in her favorite place, sprawled on top of me now, boneless and glowing, her cheek pressed to my chest. Her thighs are still trembling. I can feel the echo of every moan in the thrum of her heartbeat against mine.

I run a hand down her spine. Soft, slow. The kind of touch that says *stay*.

Then I kiss her temple.

"You're everything," I murmur, voice low and rough. "And I'm so fucking glad I caught you, little thief."

She hums against my skin. Smiles.

But then she lifts her head, meets my gaze, and her eyes are still gleaming—less with mischief now, more with something deeper.

Something that *hurts* a little, even in its beauty.

"You didn't just catch me, Dante," she says softly.

I raise a brow. "No?"

She leans in. Presses her lips to my jaw, warm and trembling.

Her voice is quieter this time. Honest.

"You ruined me." A pause. A breath. "In the best way. Just the way I needed you to."

~~~~~~~~~~~~~~~~~~~~~~~~~~

Want A Bonus Scene With Dante & Dahlia?
SIGN UP & GET IT HERE!

WANT MORE LESSONS IN DOMINANCE?

Check out the other books in this saucy series!
BOUND & BRANDED BY MAISEY YATES

Chapter One

Avery

There are two things that I'm certain of. The first is that every morning, no matter how tired I am, the sun is going to rise in the east and I'm going to have to get my ass out of bed to do the chores.

The second is that I *hate* Caleb Flynn.

I'm not exaggerating. It isn't mild dislike. It's the real deal. I *burn* with it. He's my nemesis, and has been ever since he bought that big plot of land next to ours. Ever since he built that giant, ostentatious house that stands on top of the mountain looking down on us like we're peasants and he's the king.

Though, to him, I suppose that's the reality.

I don't like change, and the first strike against him was

that he changed my daily view. No longer do I look up and see the unadulterated mountains, I also see his monstrosity of a house.

It's a beautiful house, but that's not the point. It's *different*. I get to hate it.

The second strike against him was when he bought up one hundred acres of our property. He made my dad an offer he couldn't refuse and my dad took it. I'm mad at my dad about it, too, don't worry.

I'm fair with my hatred.

At least, I like to think so.

Since he bought up that hundred acres five years ago, he's also bought fifty more. I'm struggling to keep things going while Dad refuses to give me total control, and this guy looming about all the time isn't helping.

So when I come into the house at dinnertime and he's there, the acid churn in my stomach doesn't surprise me. Doesn't even disturb me. It's all the other feelings.

Because the problem is, even though I hate Caleb Flynn from the top of his cowboy hat down to the soles of his cowboy boots, he's also as hot as the fires of the hell that I would like to send him to.

It doesn't make any logical sense. It never has. I blame that night all those years ago. He did something to me. Changed something. Something I didn't want changed.

As far as my daily life goes, I want to be in charge.

No, I *need* to be in charge.

For as long as I can remember, control has the most important thing in my life. Mainly because neither of my parents has any. I love my dad, but without me, the ranch would've fallen apart a long time ago.

Caleb leases the land he bought back to us, and he thinks that gives him the right to come here when he wants to, to weigh in on our ranching practices and in general be around when I think he has no business being here.

Caleb is... Well, he's the kind of man who thinks he's in charge of everything. He's the kind of man who thinks that the sun rises and sets on his word. No. It's going to do that regardless. One of those certainties.

Just like I'm going to keep on hating him.

"What are you doing here?" I ask.

As soon as the words exit my mouth, my dad comes in from the kitchen with two beers in his hand.

"Avery," he says. "Mr. Flynn is our guest."

I make direct eye contact with *Mr. Flynn*, those blue eyes scorching me. "Is that a fact?"

"It is," my dad says, sitting heavily in the chair next to Caleb, and handing him a beer. Caleb looks at me meaningfully as he takes a long pull from the bottle.

"I'll have the papers for you to sign by tomorrow," Caleb says.

"No!" The word explodes from my mouth. "No. You're not selling him more of our land."

"Avery..." My dad sounds exhausted, but how the fuck does he think I feel? I'm the one who runs this place. I'm the one who makes sure that we have a ranch. I manage our ranch hands and I keep up with the business aspects of it. I oversee the birthing, raising, and slaughtering of the cattle, the selling of all the meat. This is mine. My blood, my sweat, my tears—and he's been parceling the ranch out to Caleb for years.

He might not be a property developer, but as far as I'm concerned, he might as well be. He's a rhinestone cowboy if anything. Just a rich dickhead who's doing this because he can. Buying up land and not even working it.

And what's the point of that?

I'm about to say exactly that when he stands. "We'll talk more tomorrow."

He looks at me, just for a second, and everywhere his gaze touches, I burn. With fury, with something else. But it's like I can't move. Like he's immobilized me with just his glance. I hate that too.

"What are you doing?" I ask.

"Business. With your father."

He walks past me like I'm incidental. Like I don't matter. Like my feelings mean nothing. But I suppose to him my feelings don't mean a damn thing.

He walks out the front door, and I go after him.

I can hear my father's voice as I slam the door shut. No. He doesn't get to tell me what to do, not when I have to do everything. He doesn't get to exercise authority when he feels like it. Not when he can't keep the place stable without me.

"What's going on? I have a right to know. My dad's name might be on this land, but I'm the one running it."

He stops then and I keep going, bringing me almost toe to toe with him, and I can barely breathe. He's stunning, that's the problem. So tall and broad, his hair dark, and though I've rarely seen him without a hat, I know it curls just a bit at the top and around his collar. His eyes are a piercing blue I can feel all the way through my body.

He's not quick with a smile, his mouth is grim, and dark stubble covers his square jaw. He's more than classically handsome. It's almost enraging. Why should one man get wealth, strength, height and looks so fine they could topple mountains?

I'm short and poor with hard won strength in my bony arms and deeply average breasts, which as far as I'm aware is the main feature men look at – unless they're into asses. As far as your face goes, if you're competent with makeup the glitter and flash seems to read as 'beautiful' to them no matter how your features are actually arranged.

I'm bad with makeup.

And I had one man who seemed totally fine with all that and I tanked that relationship.

Caleb Flynn remains tall, gorgeous, and in my grill.

"I'm aware," he says, his gaze assessing. "Avery, you might not know anything about me, but I know everything about you. Everything about this ranch. I know what financial state you're in."

"I know that we burn through a lot of money –"

"No, you burn through money you don't have. I don't think you know how bad it is. Do you know how much your dad gambles?"

The words are like a slap. "Some."

"He's an addict."

"He's not an addict. He just… Likes to blow off a little steam."

"Avery, you're in danger of not ever having a shred of this ranch without my intervention. Luckily, I'm stepping in."

"Excuse me?"

"Your dad is borrowing money from me, but he's using the ranch as collateral."

"Are you… Are you kidding me?"

"No. I'm not."

"This is our land. You… You're a predatory son of a bitch. You've been buying off chunks of this property ever since you moved in, and this is what you've been waiting for."

"What the fuck do you think will happen if I don't intervene?" he asks, moving toward me, and I'm reminded of just how big he is. Broad, like the side of a mountain. Well over six feet.

"I don't…"

"Of course not, because you still trust him."

I scowl. "He's my father. I know he's not good with money, but I do a good job of managing this place, and we have enough."

"You don't," he says. "You, Avery Carmichael, are fucked."

The words are hard, crude and unforgiving and I find myself having to tamp down my physical reaction to them.

"Explain," I say.

"He owes people a lot of money and he hasn't been paying your mortgage. You're one more bad bet away from losing this place entirely. And not to me, to people who will put you out on the street."

I feel the blood drain from my face. "That's not true."

"It is." He laughs. "You like to think of me as a villain, but have you forgotten that I let you off the hook when you tried to burn my barn down?"

The one bad thing I ever did and he has to throw it back in my face and try to make me grateful for it.

"I haven't forgotten that you deserved it," I say.

"I could've called the police on you."

"You're welcome to do it now. I'll confess."

"No thanks. I don't have the appetite for it."

"Are you trying to act like you're being a hero?"

"No," he says. "I'm not being a hero. Though, whether you believe it or not, I actually like your father. And I don't have any desire to see the two of you out on the street. Even though you've been a pain in my ass ever since I moved up here."

"Then why are you doing this?" I ask.

"It's a good goddamned question, Avery. Maybe because you're my neighbors, and have been for five years, and it's about the longest I've ever had neighbors." He looks at me, and my whole body feels warm. "Come over tomorrow morning. We'll have a talk."

"I don't want to talk to you."

"The fact that you're standing out here running your mouth seems to suggest otherwise."

"I don't—"

"Quiet," he says. "I'm done with it. I'm done with your attitude, I'm done with you. Go inside. Come up to my place tomorrow, and we'll talk."

Something in me goes quiet, and I want to resist it. All of it. I feel myself pushing back against the need rising up inside of me to obey him.

I have to keep this sexual psychosis contained.

There's a place for it, and it's not here, not with him.

"Go inside. Be a good girl."

It's like an arrow straight between my legs. Right where I feel myself starting to ache when I look at him. I tell myself that I'm only obeying him because that's the actual surprise. That I'd do what he said instead of arguing, and I'd rather surprise him.

Then I go upstairs without speaking to my father and slam the door shut behind me.

I spend the whole rest of the night going over every problematic interaction I've ever had with him.

Caleb Flynn.

He's from here, originally. Though, I don't remember him from before. Probably because he's somewhere around fifteen years older than me, so I have no reason to. A foster kid, who went off and got rich doing something with luxury resort development. He's a billionaire. Came back and bought land looking over the town to make a point, I would think.

He moved into that big house on the hill. Then my dad sold him half our ranch. He put Dad under a lot of pressure and my mom had just left for the third and final time so it was a rough run of luck for us.

I was livid. More than that I felt reckless – something I

never was. Something I could never afford to be. But my life was falling apart and he felt like a good target for my anger.

He caught me, grabbed hold of me and slammed me up against the side of that barn, hands tight around my wrists. It had felt like a fight.

And it had felt like sex, for all an eighteen-year-old virgin could know what sex felt like.

All that rage directed against me, the fierce control of his strength. The way his large hands had directed my movements. I felt powerless.

He could have done anything he wanted to me in that moment, and instead of fear I'd felt...

Turned on.

You get the hell out of here, he'd said. *And give thanks that nobody got hurt, and that I'm not calling the police on you. You fucking brat.*

His words stuck with me. And even now, they meld into my fantasies, twisting themselves up in my head and turning into something else.

Fucking brat. He said that to me while he moved his hand from my wrist to my throat...

And I get off on that memory. Every time. Every time I see him I feel an explosion of heat that's not solely about hatred.

It fills me with shame. Then a deep sense of fear. It's what's been driving me the last few months. As pressure on the ranch has been building, it's been pushing me toward the thing I've been avoiding figuring out about myself.

Instead of sleeping I open up The Club app, which has become the dirtiest of my dirty secrets. I've been going over and over my desires for a while now. Why every interaction I have with men leaves me so unsatisfied. I blame Caleb, actually. That interaction that we had when I was young. The way he held me, the way he used his strength against me. It's like it broke something in me. Like it turned me into a monster that I don't even recognize.

And it's finally driven me to this.

There aren't very many experienced Dominants in rural Oregon.

I've been considering actually experimenting with BDSM for a while. There's no one I can talk to about it. Not here. All of my friends would be utterly and completely scandalized, and then they'd be afraid.

For me, for my sanity. Afraid I'm like my mom because obviously she's a slut and therefore I must be drawn toward slut behavior because of her.

I'd be lying if I said that didn't get twisted up inside me sometimes. As far as I know, my mom's thing isn't kink—God, I never want to know what her thing is—but it seemed like it had more to do with just wanting to get away from my dad.

But I can't deny that it puts me in a weird shame place. I tried. I tried to want a nice, normal guy who gave the potential of a nice, normal life and nice, normal sex and I blew that up three months ago.

After he proposed.

I panicked. Like a spooked horse trying to escape a barn.

I had felt like I loved John but then it just felt like more responsibility piled on top of everything I was already dealing with and I couldn't bear it. I wanted to feel like someone could take care of me, which is a simultaneously terrifying thought since I'd have to trust them in order to do that, and I don't trust anyone like that.

How can I?

Which is why this is a fantasy, though one I've been edging closer to making real. If I can pull the trigger.

My research has led me down a whole lot of rabbit holes and I've nearly leapt into a few really sketchy choices. I looked into physical sex clubs, but I don't like the idea of doing anything *in front* of anyone. Plus, I would have to travel to a bigger city and that already feels scary given that I've so rarely been outside my hometown.

I want a little secret trouble. I don't want big bad trouble where your body ends up floating in the Columbia River because you went for an orgasm and got serial killed instead. No thanks.

I've always been good. Because I *have* to be. Because if I'm not good, then the ranch is going to fall apart. My parents were dissolute and irresponsible – though to give my dad his due, he's still here.

The one time I ever misbehaved was when I sneaked onto Caleb's land and nearly burned his barn to the ground. As misbehavior went, it was relatively spectacular.

It wasn't BDSM club spectacular.

That's how I ended up finding The Club app, during a desperate Google search that went something like How Do I Find a Dom Who Won't Kill Me If I Also Don't Want to Get Railed In Front of a Room Full of Strangers.

They really do have apps for everything.

It's dedicated to helping kinky people find a partner in their area who matches their personal needs.

Everyone is vetted, their identities verified, and there's a lot of built-in protection in that. People have STD tests on file and their actual government names, even though you don't see them when you're chatting in the app.

The people running it know and if something was going to happen to you, they would know where you were and who you met with. There's just a whole lot of security built-in, and I like that.

I think.

Of course, I am also still terrified. I've only been with the one man and I assumed I'd marry him because part of me wanted to slip into an easy partnership that had some security.

The truth is, in action, I've always been the one in charge during sex too. I can't get out of my own head and I like directing things because it feels easier, safer.

The really weird thing about my BDSM fixation, my fantasies about being powerless, about being forced…is that it's nothing I've even come close to doing in real life. It's nothing I would say fits my personality at all.

BDSM is not a quick fuck. And I'm aware of that. There's something about it that terrifies me. The idea of giving my control away.

It's a particular kind of fear. One that attracts me more than it repulses me.

But the truth is, none of the sex that I've had has sparked the kind of need in me that the one angry encounter I had with Caleb has. The way he held me, his hands around my wrists like manacles. I'm intrigued by it.

I swallow hard, and open up the two Dom profiles that I've been eyeing on the app.

There's one guy who lives local who's into pain. Pain and rough sex, which intrigues me, I'm not going to lie. But it's not *quite* what I'm after.

That very thought makes me laugh at myself. What am I after? Who can say. It's not like I know.

I swipe away from that profile and look at the next. He goes by The Duke and I'm not sure if that's a John Wayne reference – which I wouldn't know if my grandma hadn't been obsessed with him – or if he's trying to get the girls who are into Bridgerton. I can't work that one out. I'm not sure I need to.

He's into bondage. Elaborate knots and a total surrender of control. Dubious consent role-play.

Every time I read those words I start getting hot.

And I am intrigued in spite of myself. Mainly because nothing scares me more than the idea of losing control, and there's something that's so attractive to me about the idea that I could flirt with a loss of control while also having all these firm agreements in place.

It feels like something I could keep control over in a way. Something that I could maintain a grip on.

Just looking at the words in his profile starts to ramp up my libido. I've messaged him twice. He knows that I live in the area and that I'm an inexperienced submissive.

He told me that he likes to train subs who are trying to get into the lifestyle.

Just that word, *training*, that should make me mad. But it doesn't.

I think about messaging him, but instead I just read over our previous interactions.

I like to train submissives. Teach them to take everything I can give. Show them their limits.

I put my hand between my legs and start to touch myself. Everything is terrible, honestly. But this fantasy, this fantasy that I will probably never act on, fuels me now. It makes me feel like everything isn't terrible.

I put my fist in my mouth as I bring myself to the peak with record speed.

God. Just thinking about him, this man that I've never seen...

It pushes me right over the edge. But I would be lying if I didn't say that I was imagining those cool blue eyes looking at me as I shudder out my orgasm.

I grit my teeth and throw my arm over my face. As long as I don't think about that tomorrow when I have to face him, I'll be fine.

Lucky, I'm practiced at that. Lucky that when I'm actually around him, the hatred usually takes over.

But for tonight, I'm just going to let myself relax into my sexual satisfaction.

I don't have anything else for me. Nothing else but this.

So I'm going to hold it close while I can.

GET BOUND & BRANDED

~~~

AFTER HOURS BY CAITLIN CREWS
Chapter One

He was there again that night, like something the dusk called up from the bay and let loose upon the gritty, crumbling city.

Calamitous villain or savior, it was hard to tell.

The man was built like some kind of modern-day Viking, what with the dark beard and those icy blue eyes. He was also one of those sculpted, muscled, *huge* men her ex-husband had liked to sneer at and call *CrossFit junkies* like that was something to be embarrassed about when *he* had liked to prance around in a lot of cycling apparel while doing very little actual cycling.

Though Joseph had known better than to sneer about anything where any of those much larger men could hear him, of course.

Romily had seen the man before. Her latter-day Viking. She had made a point of it, in fact.

Her little hideaway-from-the-whole-world boat was docked in a small, weathered marina near Brooklyn Basin in Oakland, and there were only a handful of places in the area that weren't entirely overcome by the relentless press of the streets.

Personally, Romily liked not getting shot at when she

needed a few things from the self-consciously precious little market nearby. It existed solely to cater to the fancy new high rises in the Brooklyn Basin development, all boasting some of the most beautiful views imaginable of San Francisco across the water at astronomically high prices. She even liked the absurdly uppity prices at the market—the *fact* of them, the optimism they suggested about the clientele, not actually *paying* them—and that the little boutique grocery had about seventy-five varieties of Boba, every alternative milk imaginable, and yet shockingly few actual necessities. She liked the strangeness of this new life of hers more and more—or so she told herself daily, like a mantra— so far away from what her small and claustrophobic life in Walnut Creek had become. Walnut Creek, which never had been as close to San Francisco as the people who lived there liked to pretend, and where Joseph had made certain that any friends she might have had lost touch with her completely.

He'd made certain of it but she also hadn't fought it, because surrendering to her ever-increasing isolation was easier than explaining why she was the way she had to be to survive him.

The market was one of the surprising rewards she'd found for making an entire new life for herself, unconnected to anyone or anything she'd known before, in a place no one who'd ever met her would think to look for her.

Another was *him*. The man.

Her bearded, mouthwateringly well-cut Viking who was usually in what she'd originally thought was a garage, thanks to its roll-up metal door covered with the expected spray-painted tags. It sat between a bizarre sort of down-market seafood restaurant that did a surprising amount of business, given the often questionable neighborhood there on the Embarcadero, and a seedy though not wholly terrifying dive bar. The bar came alive only late at night and often left its patrons worse for wear as well as targets for petty thieves as they stumbled off along the waterfront path that stretched all the way to Jack London Square.

And it turned out it wasn't a garage. Romily had found that out one very early morning when she couldn't sleep and so was out walking. An activity that was not as relaxing as she'd hoped, given what lurked in the shadows beneath the palm trees here, but it was a lot better than her nightmares.

She'd heard the noise before she'd understood what she was hearing, odd metallic crashes and a kind of growling through the morning fog, making her wonder if she'd been about to encounter another monster she would have to run from.

Or, more worryingly, if maybe it was time she ran *toward* the monster instead, because there was something almost exhilarating in the thought of *choosing* it—

But there were no monsters. Not the kind that chased her, anyway.

It was a gym.

One of those gyms with black floors and horrible, shouty music, filled with terrifying equipment like bags hanging from chains like some kind of fitness abattoir—without a single soothing elliptical machine or smoothie counter to be seen.

What it had was *him*.

Sometimes other big, scary men were there too. They all looked like they were trying to make themselves into his clones, but never quite got there. There were a lot of bearded, tattooed, grim-eyed men in that dark little place, all crashing weights and grunting noises, but only *he* seemed to disturb the air when he moved.

And that was hard to do in this part of Oakland, where *disturbance* was just regular, daily background noise.

Those disturbances were why Romily didn't love leaving

her boat. Well. One reason, anyway. If she could, she'd stay hidden away in the marina night and day, but even someone who wanted to stay anonymous and forever unfound had to go out sometimes.

So every day, Romily made herself leave the marina and walk around, because that was what people were supposed to do, and she was trying her best to do that. To *people* like she really was a person and not just the ruined, bombed-out shell of a person her ex had made her.

And not only when the nightmares had her waking up choking again.

After that first morning, in the fog, she'd made it a point to learn the hours of the gym—and they weren't posted anywhere she could see. Apparently you had to have a beard and a certain grimness to you to work it out.

Or you had to live nearby, like Romily.

By now she had managed to see him at almost all times of day.

There was usually a t-shirt situation but on really good days, he was shirtless. Curling things. Slamming things. Sometimes running with all his sleek muscles on display, not to mention the kind of tattoos that had always fascinated her, all over his skin like spells and incantations. Sometimes at night she would lie in her berth and trace the patterns she saw inked into his skin all over her own body.

Sometimes she would slide her hands between her legs and let her imagination go wild—

Tonight, though, he surprised her.

Shocked her, even.

Because tonight she saw him when she hadn't expected it. When she wasn't looking for him, for a change.

He was walking out on the commons—the public park behind the old Port of Oakland building that offered dreamy views over the estuary and further on toward San Francisco.

He was just *there*, like he wasn't a gorgeous, terrifying warrior of a man, out in the falling dusk. As if he was *normal* instead of *extraordinary*, out here in public surrounded by regular people, and Romily didn't know what to do with herself.

She barely knew who she was. She almost swallowed her own tongue. She was certainly holding her breath.

She froze, right in the middle of a stream of people, which was a good way to get trampled.

But she couldn't move.

It was a small miracle that there was a knot of skateboarders between them. Not that he would recognize her. Why would he? But she was sure he'd notice someone frozen solid and *gaping* at him.

It was a kind of miracle to see him like this. Just... out.

No crashing weights or music ripe with full-throated bellows and dark, hot baselines designed to disturb.

Just a powerfully built man prowling his way down a walkway.

He was mesmerizing.

He wasn't wearing the things he usually did in the gym. He was in jeans that made a grand feast out of the powerful muscles of his quads and ass. He wore a black Henley that only emphasized his outrageously cut arms. He wore a dark knitted beanie like every other bearded dude in the East Bay, but he was nothing like any of *them*.

Something about *him* made her bones hum and her body ache.

Like a good fever, if that was a thing.

Long after he'd walked off, back to whatever life he must lead and she should probably wonder about that at some point, Romily stayed frozen still. She didn't move even when the skateboarders looped all around her like she was a new obstacle for them to conquer.

She didn't move for so long that when she did, she felt stiff and something like sore.

In her chest, where the heart she'd written off as defective suddenly decided to start beating again, too hard and too jagged.

Hours later, instead of walking straight to the marina entrance and hurrying down the dock to the safety of her boat, she looped around on the walkway instead. She told herself she was simply enjoying a nightly walk—not something she normally indulged in this far from dawn, not least because it could get a bit nutty out here in the dark— but that wasn't entirely true.

Romily was deliberately taking another pass near the gym.

Just in case, she told herself.

Just in case what? she asked herself a bit scornfully. *He's standing around outside a gym on a Friday night? Just to see if he can cause a commotion?*

Not likely.

When she headed toward his gym, she saw that the garage door was closed. Not a surprise.

That there was a light on inside, though, was. She could see it through the cracks in the small, barred windows in the rolling garage door. Just a hint of light, peeking out into the dark.

Romily wasn't usually out this late, or for so long, but a lot of other people were because it was a Friday. And the weather was beautiful. There had been fleets of kayaks in the estuary all day. The restaurant was packed and loud. There were even people waiting in line to get into the dive bar.

She had gone out tonight as a test. There had been music in the park, so she'd gone over to listen. Once she'd *unstuck* herself that was. She'd watched people dance. Sing. Roller blade through the evening. She'd made herself sit there in a crowd, like normal people did, even in this part of beleaguered Oakland.

But all the while she'd daydreamed about *him.*

Now she wanted nothing but to get to her boat and hide away again, so she could lie in her cozy berth and go over every detail of his pecs straining beneath that Henley, then make up some delicious scenarios to go with it, but that light taunted her.

Romily made her way past the crowd outside the bar, then did something she'd never done before. She didn't overthink it. She had a crazy little idea and she went with it. Instead of walking her usual path past the front of the gym and on to the marina's gated entrance, she slipped into the alley between it and the bar.

She felt breathless. Audacious.

Like the girl she'd almost been before Joseph had gotten his hooks in her.

Thinking about Joseph was galvanizing, because he would hate this. All of this. That she was in this part of Oakland. That she lived on a boat of questionable seaworthiness. That she was having *whole thoughts and a life* without his permission and direction.

Not to mention that she noticed other men at all, much less one who looked like a Viking god.

He would make her pay for all of that. She knew that all too well. She'd lived it for longer than she liked to think about—

But Joseph wasn't here.

So Romily walked faster and with more determination into the dark, until the shadows swallowed her up.

And when she got farther still, she saw that there were stairs that led up to a higher floor above the gym. But beneath it was another door, with an actual name on it:

LONDON'S. With a list of hours and a phone number etched beneath.

Like it was a real gym after all, not just a home away from home for Vikings lost in time.

But Romily didn't care about any of that, not at the moment, because she could see through the glass.

He was there. Right there, in what looked like some kind of front desk area, though she could barely concentrate on the details.

Because he wasn't doing paperwork.

He had a blonde woman bent over that desk and he was fucking her.

Hard.

GET AFTER HOURS

HARD DISCIPLINE BY JACKIE ASHENDEN

ACKNOWLEDGMENTS

What happens when you have a gaggle of author friends who love spicy romance, have fifteen minutes to spare on a WhatsApp Group, and one starts a post with a... "hey, how about we....?"

I'll give you three...no four guesses, haha!

Thank you Maisey Yates, Caitlin Crews and Jackie Ashenden for this saucy , fun ride into The Club world (No, this is not a British Airways plug!). Our little adventure has been a blast! Can't wait to see what we do next!

ABOUT THE AUTHOR

Want updates on book news and bonus reads?
JOIN MY NEWSLETTER

Or come say hi on social media!

ALSO BY ZARA COX

MILE HIGH ADDICTION
SKY HIGH OBSESSION
SEVEN NIGHT STOPOVER

Did you know I also write contemporary romance as Maya Blake?
Check out my latest book!
THE FORGOTTEN WIFE

Printed in Dunstable, United Kingdom